Rebellious Highland Hearts

SHORT STORY COLLECTION

JAYNE CASTEL

All characters and situations in this publication are fictitious, and any resemblance to living persons is purely coincidental.

Rebellious Highland Hearts: Short Story Collection, by Jayne Castel

Copyright © 2024 by Jayne Castel. All rights reserved. No part of this publication may be reproduced, stored in a retrieval system, or transmitted in any form or by any means—electronic, mechanical, recording, or otherwise—without the prior written permission of the author.

Published by Winter Mist Press

Edited by Tim Burton
Cover images generated by Midjourney.
Cover design by Winter Mist Press

Visit Jayne's website: www.jaynecastel.com

Contents

WOOING THE ALEWIFE......................4

HEART OF ICE....................................31

HEART OF FIRE..................................59

DIVE INTO MY BACKLIST!.......................85

ABOUT THE AUTHOR........................86

WOOING THE ALEWIFE

A REBELLIOUS HIGHLAND HEARTS SHORT STORY

THE HANDCART LURCHED to a halt. Turning, to see that the small wooden wagon had listed sideways, causing the barrel she'd been towing home to topple over, Eara Mackay issued a salty curse.

She'd only had that infernal wheel mended a few months earlier. Dun Ugadale didn't have a wainwright—the nearest tradesman skilled in repairing carts and wagons was in Ceann Locha—and so she'd asked the elderly village ironmonger instead to replace the rusted pin and help her remount the left wheel. Auld Finlay was losing his sight, and his fingers were swollen with use and age. He'd done his best—only it wasn't good enough.

Muttering more curses, Eara let go of the rope she'd been towing the cart with and stalked around to inspect the damage.

It was a drizzly morning in late August, and there was a bite to the air, hinting that autumn approached. She'd been traveling down a narrow path that led from the spring located to the southwest of Dun Ugadale and had almost reached the rocky outcrop where the broch perched.

The clouds had lowered this afternoon though, obscuring the high lichen-and-moss-encrusted walls from view.

Fortunately, Eara had stoppered the barrel. Using spring water, rather than the brackish water from the village well, made a huge difference to the taste of the ale she brewed. Her frequent trips to the spring were time-consuming yet essential. And this was the only cart she owned.

Staring at where the wheel sat at an odd angle, Eara balled her hands into fists at her sides.

Curse this rickety cart to Hades, she was tired to the marrow of dealing with obstacle after obstacle.

She hadn't been happily wed to James, yet he'd taken care of any problems that arose with the business. She hadn't realized just how much responsibility he'd shouldered until she found herself alone after his death. Her friend Rose often helped her in the mornings with the brewing of ale, but there was so much she still had to cope with alone.

Her frustration spilled over into anger then, and she let out a string of the filthiest curses she knew and kicked the wheel.

Pain exploded in her toes, and she yelled out. She was wearing worn leather boots, but the impact jarred her toes nonetheless. Hopping around on one foot, she continued to swear.

"God's blood, woman … ye are making enough noise to raise the dead."

Eara's cursing choked off, and, still standing like a crane on one leg, she glanced over her shoulder to see a man on horseback rein in behind her.

Kyle MacAlister's moss-green eyes twinkled in amusement as he watched her.

Moments passed, and then a grin stretched the bailiff's face.

"Find my predicament amusing, do ye?" Eara shot back, indignant. It was fortunate that she liked the bailiff, or she'd have snarled at him.

Kyle shook his head before swinging down from his horse. "I thought I told ye months ago to get that wheel mended?"

"I did," she replied ungraciously, wincing as she placed her bruised foot on the ground and gingerly tested her weight upon it. "But Auld Finlay's eyesight isn't the best these days."

"There's a good wainwright in Ceann Locha."

Eara stiffened. "I'm aware of that," she replied with a sigh. "But how was I ever going to get my cart down to him?" *Or afford to pay him*, she added silently.

Kyle met her eye then. "Ye could have asked me to help," he pointed out gently. "Ye know I would have."

Their gazes held for a few moments before Eara cut hers away, embarrassed.

Aye, she was aware of the bailiff's interest in her.

After coming to her rescue earlier in the year, the last time the wheel had come off her handcart, he'd then visited her bothy a few days later to buy some ale. It was a sunny eve, so they'd sat outside in the garden for a short while before he went on his way. He'd then asked her to dance at Beltaine, and although she'd enjoyed the experience, and the flirting that had gone along with it, Eara had deliberately kept her distance from Dun Ugadale's bailiff ever since.

With long brown hair and laughing green eyes, Kyle was attractive enough to turn many a lass's head. His close-cropped beard emphasized the strength of his jaw, and Eara had found herself admiring his tall and rangy frame when they'd danced together.

He was just the sort of man she'd enjoy a tumble with, just the sort of man she could lose her wits over.

But ever since James's death, she'd been careful with men. She lived alone in the bothy she and her husband had once shared and had several nosy neighbors. She sold ale to some folk directly from her door, as well as at the twice-weekly markets, and didn't want to get a reputation for selling other 'favors' as well. Her rapport with many of the villagers had been tense over the summer, while Father Gregor had lived among them, and she was wary of providing fodder for the gossips.

"Come on, Eara," the bailiff said, breaking the silence between them. "Let's see if we can get yer cart on the road again."

Nodding, Eara stepped back to allow him to approach the wheel. "Ye seem to be making a habit of coming to my aid," she noted.

"I wouldn't call 'twice' a habit," he replied. "But luckily for ye, I've business with the laird this afternoon."

Hunkering down, Kyle inspected the wheel. He then reached behind it and plucked something out of the dirt. "It's the same problem as before … the pin has come loose." His gaze narrowed. "As I warned ye, the axle is rusted … the pin will keep falling out as it worsens. The whole thing needs replacing."

Eara drew in a deep breath and tried to ignore the tightening in her chest. She couldn't afford that.

"I'll need ye to lift the cart, lass," Kyle said then, "but first, I'll get this barrel off so ye don't hurt yer back."

"Don't bother," she muttered. "I'm strong enough to lift the cart." And she was. Eara was used to heaving sacks and barrels on a daily basis. To prove her point, she moved to the rear of the cart and raised the base up.

A moment later, Kyle had slid the wheel back on and secured the pin. "That'll do for now," the bailiff announced, wiping his hands upon his braies. "But it needs the wainwright's skill." He paused then, his gaze flicking over her face. "I'll take ye, if ye like?"

Eara swallowed, wishing the man would drop the subject. "That's kind of ye, Kyle ... but coin is tight at present. It'll have to wait."

His brow furrowed, and he took a step toward her. "Is business not thriving?"

"Well enough ... things are certainly better now that Father Gregor has gone."

The bailiff pulled a face at the mention of the troublemaking priest. "I know he turned folk against Rose ... but not ye too?"

"Aye, well, I'm an alewife ... we're strange women, didn't ye know? Not to be trusted. When Maisie MacDonald and her friends turned against Rose, many locals stopped buying from me." Eara halted there, her mouth pursing. "And although most of my customers have returned, the hefty price of barley makes it difficult to carve out a living."

Kyle inclined his head. "Ye brew the best ale I've ever tasted, Eara." There wasn't a trace of teasing in his voice now. "It would be shame to see ye shut up shop."

Eara gave a soft snort, even as warmth flushed through her. His words were kind and appreciated, yet they didn't change anything. With another sigh, she moved around to the front of the cart and picked up the rope. "I'd better get on … and *ye* shouldn't keep Iver Mackay waiting."

"He can wait," the bailiff replied. "Here, ye lead my horse, and I shall tow the cart for ye."

Heat rolled over Eara. The man's gallantry was starting to embarrass her. "There's no need. I can—"

"There's no doubt ye are a capable woman," Kyle interrupted smoothly. "But that doesn't mean ye have to do everything on yer own. Here … give me that rope."

Jaw clenched, Eara complied. It was clear the bailiff was as stubborn as her and wasn't going to give up.

They swapped sides, and she took the reins of his stocky dun gelding.

Together, they headed off down the narrow path, circuiting the rocky outcrop. Presently, the path took them past the kirk. The surrounding graveyard was wreathed in mist, and the pitched roof of the kirk pierced the low cloud. It looked empty, forlorn, this afternoon.

"Has the laird found a new priest yet?" Kyle asked. Like Eara, he was surveying the kirk as they passed by.

"Rose told me they've found one … although he's coming from Inverness. Father Euan should be here within a month."

"Well, let's hope he's a kindly soul like Father Ross then. We don't need another bigot amongst us."

"Aye," she agreed with a decisive nod. "I look forward to being able to attend services again."

"I usually go to the kirk in Ceann Locha with my bairns every Sunday," Kyle said with a smile. "Although they complain that Father Macum is dull enough to rot yer thought cage."

Eara laughed. "Aye, I'd heard as much." She eyed him then. "I'd forgotten ye have bairns."

His mouth quirked. "Aye, three wee lassies. I have help raising them, for my brother and his wife share our cottage … but they can be a handful all the same." His usually merry gaze shadowed then. "They've all grown a little wild after their mother died."

"How long ago did ye lose her?" Eara asked. In truth, she often forgot that Kyle was a widower too, for he had a cheerful manner and didn't seem embittered the way some men became when they lost their wives.

"Two and a half years now," he replied. "Freya and I both indulged our daughters … although the bairns have inherited their Ma's strong will."

Something tugged at Eara then, regret and sadness. She and James were wed over five years, yet her womb had never quickened. She'd longed to have a bairn but had told herself it wasn't meant to be.

"I can tell from yer face that they bring ye joy," she murmured.

His mouth curved, even if sadness still lingered in his eyes. "More than words can say."

They walked in silence then, making their way through the village to the small bothy where Eara lived. A sign hung from the gate, with a broomstick etched upon it—the mark of an alewife's residence.

Handing the bailiff his horse, Eara met his eye. "Thank ye, once again, Kyle, for yer help."

He winked at her. "It's always a pleasure, lass."

Eara snorted, folding her arms across her chest. She wanted to think of a witty response, yet couldn't. The bailiff had a way of unbalancing her. Instead, she watched as Kyle moved around and mounted his horse once more. Then, gathering the reins, he met her eye. "My offer to take yer cart to the wainwright still stands."

Eara tensed, shaking her head. "Thank ye, but—"

"Why don't ye allow me to cover the cost of the repairs … ye can repay the debt in ale, if ye like?"

Eara's stomach clenched. The man was like a dog with a bone. She could tell he wasn't going to let the matter drop. However, ever since James's death, she'd been wary of accepting 'help' from men. It often came with an expectation she would allow them to woo her, or that she'd offer them sexual favors. "Yer kindness is noted," she replied, reaching for the gate. "But I must decline."

Kyle cocked an eyebrow. "Just think on it, Eara. Promise me that."

Eara huffed a sigh. Surely, he'd forget his offer with the passing of the days. She'd be wise to appease him so he'd let the matter drop. "Very well."

"Fresh ale!" Eara called out. "Just half a penny to fill two skins!"

"Go on then." A squat, balding man with a paunch halted before her stall and reached into the leather pack he carried. "Fill these up."

"Good day, Bruce," she replied with a relieved smile. It had been a slow morning, and she still had three-quarters of a barrel of ale perched on the trestle table next to her.

The twice-weekly market took place in the village square, a cluster of stalls selling fresh produce, eggs, cheese, meat, and livestock.

Eara was the only one selling ale, yet that didn't make plying her trade any easier.

"How's yer wife these days?" she asked the farmer. Bruce MacDonald worked fields just south of the village, although his wife had taken poorly of late. The woman was afflicted with stiff and aching joints, and barely left the house.

Bruce sighed, making it clear that the situation hadn't improved. "She gets by, lass … thank ye for asking."

Eara took the two empty bladders he passed her and filled them. She'd just stoppered the second when she spied a tall man with long brown hair and a short beard making his way through the crowd toward her.

He held the hands of two bairns and carried the third upon his shoulders.

Eara's foolish heart kicked hard in her chest.

It had been nearly a week since she'd seen Kyle MacAlister last, yet she hadn't expected to encounter him at the market. The bailiff didn't usually attend, and she'd never seen him with his daughters before.

The lasses all had impish faces and wild brown hair like their father's. Yet, as they drew near, she saw that only the youngest had his green eyes. The two eldest had eyes the color of oak.

"Here ye are, lass." The farmer pressed a half penny into her hand. "I'll see ye next week."

"Ye will, Bruce," Eara replied, pretending she hadn't seen the bailiff's approach. "Give my best to Fiona, as always."

The farmer loaded the two skins into his pack and moved off, just as Kyle stopped before her stall.

Eara shifted uncomfortably, resisting the urge to smooth the apron she had on over her kirtle or to adjust the tall pointed cloth hat she always wore to market—one that distinguished her from the other stallholders.

The family were all dressed well, and she felt a little shabby in comparison.

However, Kyle didn't appear to care, for he flashed her a wide smile. "Eara … may I introduce ye to Bridget, Mairi, and Una."

All three lasses studied her with wide eyes and solemn faces.

"Good morning," she greeted them with an embarrassed smile.

"Good morn," one of them—who appeared the youngest, perched upon Kyle's shoulders—chirped, while the other two favored her with bashful smiles of their own. "Ye have pretty hair," the lass added then. "It's the color of straw."

Eara smiled. "Thank ye … Una?"

"Are we buying ale, Da?" Another sister asked then.

"Aye, Bridget." The bailiff unslung a bag from his back and passed it to Eara. "There's four skins in there to fill, if ye please."

Eara nodded, relieved he was here to purchase from her and not to flirt. It wouldn't be right anyway, not with his daughters listening in.

She got to work filling the skins, aware that Kyle and his daughters were all watching her.

She was halfway through filling the second when he cleared his throat. "Have ye thought on my offer?"

Heat flushed over Eara. Aye, she had. Constantly. Pride warred with necessity. She needed that handcart, and the bailiff didn't seem the sort to take advantage of a woman on her own.

Even so, after James, she was weary of giving any man something to hold over her. She hated how dependent she'd become on him during their marriage, and how he'd used it to control her. Life was far harder these days, yet at least she didn't have to tell anyone where she was going or how long she'd be there. She didn't need to worry about having supper on the table at a certain hour or fear that she'd offended her man.

James had often sulked for days if she displeased him. It had become wearying indeed. After his death, she'd been plagued with guilt—as, although she'd loved her husband, she found she didn't *miss* him.

"I have," she said after a lengthy pause. "Does it still stand?"

Their gazes met, and his mouth curved. "Aye."

Eara sighed. "Well then, I accept."

"Good." His gaze never left her face as his smile widened. Eara's breathing grew shallow. Lord, had she made a mistake in agreeing to this? The man was too comely by half. "I shall fetch ye and the cart tomorrow morning, shortly after dawn."

Kyle MacAlister was a man of his word. Shortly after the rooster in Eara's garden crowed, the bailiff appeared at her gate.

Emerging from her bothy, with a woolen shawl about her shoulders, for the morning was cool, Eara's gaze traveled to the wagon behind him, and the garron drawing it.

She'd expected to see him on horseback.

Her surprise must have shown on her face, for Kyle flashed her one of his disarming smiles. "It'll be easier if we load yer cart onto my wool wagon … this way, ye can spare yer legs the walk too."

Eara found herself smiling back. She wasn't afraid of a long walk, although the journey to Ceann Locha, and back again in one day, was a tiring one. She appreciated the gesture.

"Very well," she replied. "Let's fetch my cart and be on our way."

A short while later, they were rattling down the road out of the village, around the eastern walls of the broch, and heading south along the coast. It was a road that Eara had taken many a time, although it was a while since she'd traveled like this, sitting on a wagon.

She and Kyle perched up front, while he held the reins. There wasn't much space, and they sat with their thighs touching. The heat of his legs against hers was both exciting and disconcerting. Yet if Kyle was affected by their proximity, he didn't let on.

"The morning air is getting a bite to it," he noted as a sea breeze whipped around them off Kilbrannan Sound.

"Aye." Eara drew her shawl closer still, glad for the warmth his nearness afforded her. She had a slight frame and had always felt the cold. "I never look forward to winter."

"Few of us do," he replied. "Although, since I left my brother to the sheep farming so I could work as Mackay's bailiff, the cold months haven't bothered me as much as they used to."

Eara eyed him. "So, ye enjoy yer new position then?"

"Well enough."

"Even when ye have to threaten folk who won't pay their rents?"

He snorted. "Is that what ye think I do?"

She favored him with an arch look. "No one looks forward to a visit from the bailiff."

He gave her a slow smile in response. "Even *ye*, Eara?"

There was an intimacy in his tone, an undercurrent of sensuality, that made her pulse quicken. Aye, there was no denying she was attracted to him. She had been for a while now. Whenever their paths crossed, they often enjoyed light-hearted banter. Yet underneath, there was a tension between them, an awareness, that was steadily growing with each encounter.

He felt it, and so did she.

"The arrogance of ye," she muttered with a toss of her head, doing her best to ignore her body's reaction to him. "Don't ye get to thinking I sit around waiting for ye to turn up at my door."

"I know ye aren't the sort of woman to pine over a man or to sit idle," he replied, still smiling. "But do ye like it when I visit?"

"Maybe," she said lightly.

His smile widened in response.

"This will take me a few days to mend," the wainwright announced, after looking at the handcart. "The axle needs to be completely replaced."

Eara sighed. She'd suspected as much. Her belly tightened. How much was this going to cost Kyle?

"Send word to me once it's done, Fergus," the bailiff said. "Do ye need part payment now?"

The wainwright shook his head, his craggy face splitting into a smile. "No, when I'm done will suffice. I know ye always pay up, lad."

Leaving the wainwright's workshop, Eara glanced over at him. "Ye should have asked him how much it would be."

He raised an eyebrow. "Why?"

"I don't want him charging ye too much."

"He won't. Fergus and I are good friends."

Eara nodded, although she still wasn't happy about this. Reaching up, she massaged a tense muscle in her shoulder.

"Don't look so worried, lass." Kyle stepped close, crooking a finger lightly under her chin so that she met his gaze. "Ye need that cart to be sturdy … for yer livelihood."

"But how am I supposed to repay ye?"

The old fears were rising, choking her. Yet the feel of his hand on her skin was distracting. She found herself staring at his mouth. His bottom lip was fuller than his top one, with a sensual curve she suddenly wanted to explore.

Stop it, she chastised herself. Such thoughts would lead her into trouble.

"I told ye … some ale free of charge every week will be sufficient."

"That could take a while to repay."

His gaze held hers. "I'm not in any hurry." He paused then, removing his finger from under her chin. "Are ye?"

Eara swallowed. "No," she whispered.

"Then there isn't a problem, is there?" He took her arm and looped it through his, leading her down the street and back to Ceann Locha's busy port. "Come, noon approaches. Let's get ourselves something to eat at the *Ardshiel Tavern*, and then I'll take ye home."

Seated opposite each other at a corner table as they ate roast mutton and freshly baked bread, washed down with a tankard of ale, Eara and Kyle conversed like old friends.

He told her of how his late wife, Freya, had been his childhood sweetheart. They'd both wed at seventeen, although it had been a few years before she'd had her first child.

The lung sickness that had taken his wife had driven a spike through his happy existence. Indeed, his daughters had taken Freya's death better than Kyle did, for they had the love of their father, aunt, and uncle to help them recover from their grief. However, Kyle struggled. Sheep farming lost its appeal soon after, which was why he'd been relieved when Iver Mackay offered him a job. He'd been in need of a fresh start.

In turn, Eara admitted that she'd felt guilty after James died. His death had been sudden, a drowning when he'd been out fishing on the sound with his brother, but once the shock had passed, relief had filled her.

"He could be … controlling," Eara said softly, dropping her gaze to her tankard, where she swirled the dregs of her ale. It was good, although a little bitterer than the ale she brewed. "But I didn't realize how suffocated I felt until after he was gone." She glanced up to find Kyle watching her. His expression was unusually serious, and she tensed. "Does that make me a bad woman?"

He raised his eyebrows. "No."

"But a widow should miss her husband. I didn't. At night, I found myself thanking the Lord that I was free."

"Ye were young when ye wed, Eara. Ye can be forgiven for realizing ye'd chosen badly only after it was too late. Ye wouldn't be the first." He leaned back in his chair, regarding her, his gaze hooding. "But not all men try to crush a woman's spirit, ye know?"

Eara's heart did a little flutter. "Don't they?"

In her experience, they often did. Her parents were both dead, carried away by fevers nearly a decade earlier, yet she remembered how dominant her father had been, and how cowed her mother was. Her friend Rose had once been terribly put upon by her menfolk, although she was now blissfully happy with Kerr Mackay, the Captain of the Dun Ugadale Guard. Rose had told her that Kerr treated her as his equal in all things. Indeed, Eara had been surprised when he didn't seem bothered about the fact that Rose spent most mornings helping Eara with her work. All the same, Eara thought their relationship an exception.

"No," Kyle replied gently. "Some want a partner to share life's ups and downs with … to chase away the loneliness of long winter nights. Someone to worry about and look out for." He broke off then before giving her a small, slightly embarrassed, smile. "I know I do."

It was growing late in the afternoon when they reached Dun Ugadale village. The days were shortening now, and the brisk breeze of earlier in the day had turned colder still. Dark clouds raced across the sky, promising rain to come.

The worsening weather didn't bother Eara though. She'd felt lighthearted all the way home. Thanks to the bailiff, her handcart was being fixed properly. The wainwright had promised them that the cart would be ready in a few days, and Kyle had offered to go with her to retrieve it.

"Ye have helped me greatly today, Kyle," she murmured, as she climbed down from the wagon. "Thank ye."

"My pleasure, lass."

Their gazes met, and Eara sucked in a deep breath before exhaling slowly. "Since I'm repaying ye in ale, would ye like to come in for some supper? I might as well feed ye too."

She'd been working up to this invitation the entire ride back from Ceann Locha and had finally gotten up the courage to issue it. However, she'd spoken with casual indifference, as if it mattered not to her if he refused. The bailiff lived a short ride south of the broch, and she imagined he was now weary and keen to return home to his brood.

She braced herself for his refusal, surprised when he replied, "Aye, Eara … thank ye."

"Ye aren't missing yer daughters?" she asked, a challenge creeping into her voice.

Kyle met her eye. "I always miss them when I'm away … but their aunt will ensure they're fed and tucked safely in bed this eve." He paused then, his mouth quirking. "Besides, when a beautiful woman invites me to supper, I'd be a fool to refuse."

Their gazes held, and Eara's pulse quickened. "Ye have a way with words, Kyle MacAlister," she murmured. "My mother always told me to be wary of men with gilded tongues."

He snorted. "She must have been cynical … there's nothing wrong with complimenting a woman." He paused then, his gaze still holding hers. "As long as it's sincere."

Warmth flowered around Eara, creeping up her neck as she turned and pushed open the gate.

Kyle led his pony and cart inside her garden, unshackling the garron and tying it to an apple tree. Meanwhile, Eara got to work indoors, lighting the second of the two hearths inside her bothy.

The first hearth, the largest, had a large cauldron perched atop it. That was where she brewed her ale. The second fire pit, much smaller, had a couple of stools next to it; this was where Eara cooked her meals.

The musty smell of grain filled her cottage, from the sacks of barley that sat neatly against one wall. As Eara struck her flint, watching as golden sparks landed on the tinder she'd set, something warm and sinuous wrapped itself around her ankles. Glancing down, her gaze settled on Ember, her cat.

"Good eve, lass," Eara murmured, stroking the cat's back. "Missed me, did ye?"

"That's a well-fed feline," Kyle noted as he entered the bothy, ducking his head to avoid cracking it on the lintel.

"Aye," Eara chucked the portly black cat affectionately under the chin. "It's all the rodents she catches in here. An alewife can't be without her faithful mouser." The fire caught then, tender red-gold flames flickering up and illuminating the shadowy interior. Glancing up, she noted that Kyle was observing her cottage. Of course, even though he'd bought ale from her door a few times, she'd never actually invited him inside.

Her cheeks warmed then, and she wondered what he thought of it. "It's humble, I know," she murmured.

"Aye … but well-kept," he replied, meeting her eye. "Yer home is welcoming, Eara."

Her mouth curved. She'd done her best with what she had over the years. Hangings made of dyed sheepskin covered the mud and stone walls, and bunches of dried herbs and flowers hung from the rafters. Despite that she stored the sacks of barley she used for brewing in here, she tried to keep her living space tidy. Now that she was satisfied her mistress was home, Ember had curled up in a basket near the hanging that shielded the sleeping alcove from view.

It pleased Eara more than she expected that Kyle liked her bothy.

Putting more twigs on the fire, she watched as the small brick of peat she'd placed in the center of the hearth started to smolder. "Supper will be simple, I'm afraid," she announced, rising to her feet. "I hope ye like oatcakes, cheese, and dried sausage?"

Leaning against the doorframe, arms folded as he watched her, Kyle smiled. "My favorite."

Eara raised an eyebrow. She was sure it wasn't.

She moved across to a workbench to the right of the door and opened a wooden bread box, extracting the oatcakes she'd made the evening before. They kept well for a few days so would be fresh enough to serve to guests.

"Can I help?" Kyle asked.

Eara cut him a surprised look. "How?"

He gestured to the wheel of cheese she'd just taken down from a high shelf. "Shall I cut a wedge or two from that?"

Eara inclined her head, not sure she'd heard him correctly. In all her years with James, he'd never once offered to help her prepare meals. Her first urge was to brush his offer away, yet she checked it.

Let him assist—it would mean they'd eat sooner.

Nodding, she indicated to a knife hanging on the wall. "Thank ye."

They worked together at the bench, preparing two wooden trenchers with food. They didn't speak, yet it was a companionable silence.

I could get used to this, Eara thought before catching herself. She was starved of male company indeed if a little kindness had her going weak at the knees.

Eara poured them each a cup of ale before they took their trenchers across to the fire. There they ate their suppers, with their food perched on their knees, their cups of ale by their sides.

Kyle ate heartily, enjoying the simple meal. Taking a sip from his cup, he then sighed. "Ye really do make the best ale on the Kintyre peninsula, lass."

Eara huffed a laugh. "That's quite a claim, MacAlister. Have ye sampled all of them?"

"My new job takes me quite a distance," he replied, his green eyes twinkling. "Ye would be surprised how many alehouses I've visited over the past year." He paused then, his expression sobering. "I'm in earnest though … ye have a rare talent."

Eara shrugged. "Perhaps … although I do find the job wearying at times."

He nodded. "It's a lot for a woman alone to shoulder."

"Rose helps out," she replied hurriedly, suddenly defensive. "That eases my workload, a little."

"Aye, but if ye had a husband working at yer side, ye would have less to worry about."

Eara's gaze narrowed. "Would I?"

He continued to hold her gaze, unbothered by the challenge in her voice. "Aye, ye would." Kyle put aside his trencher and drained the last of his ale. He then leaned forward, his expression intense in the flickering firelight. "I know ye are wary of shackling yerself to anyone again … to have any man become yer master … but what if ye found a husband who wanted to work alongside ye, someone who had no interest in dominating ye or turning ye into his servant?"

Eara's pulse fluttered. "Such a man doesn't exist," she scoffed, trying to mask her reaction to his words and the intensity of his gaze. She too had finished her meal and had been nursing her cup of ale, although her fingers now tightened around it.

"Aye, he does," Kyle replied softly. "He's sitting right in front of ye, lass."

Eara wanted to give a rude snort, to wave away his declaration with her hand. But she found she couldn't.

The air between them crackled as if a summer storm were about to unleash itself overhead.

Inhaling shakily, she fought the urge to drop her gaze and stare intently at the fire instead.

"Is that an offer of marriage?" she asked finally, breaking the silence between them.

"Aye," he said huskily. "I want to be part of yer life, Eara. What would ye say to letting me share this cottage with ye?"

Her lips parted, her breath gusting out of her. "But what about yer daughters?"

"They'd live here … with us."

An incredulous snort did escape then. "This bothy is far too small for a family."

"Ye have a large garden, Eara … I can extend this dwelling and make it suitable for all of us."

Eara lifted her cup to her lips and drained the rest of her ale in a couple of gulps. Lord, she needed something to fortify herself right now. "It sounds as if ye have already thought on all of this at length," she said, her tone sharpening. "Ye say ye don't wish to control me, but ye are already making plans on my behalf."

His jaw tightened. "That's not the truth. I'm just speaking plainly. I have three daughters, Eara. I would never leave them behind."

"I wasn't asking ye to."

"Ye would make a fine mother."

Something fluttered deep inside her ribs at these words. A long-suppressed desire for family and belonging. Eara quashed it. "Maybe, but is that how ye see me, as the woman who will take care of yer brood, who'll wash yer braies? There was I thinking ye were silver-tongued. I clearly was mistaken."

Kyle made an exasperated sound in the back of his throat. "No, I—"

"Enough of this talk." Eara set her cup down and rose to her feet. "God's teeth, MacAlister. Ye haven't even kissed me, and ye are talking about moving yer daughters in here. I think it's time ye—"

"I can remedy that, lass." Eara never finished her sentence, for Kyle launched himself off his stool, stepped around the hearth, and hauled her into his arms.

An instant later, his mouth crashed down on hers, swallowing her indignance.

The kiss was fierce, bruising, and once the jolt of shock passed, Eara reacted.

No, she didn't shove him back and slap his face. It wasn't anger that barreled into her, but wild, stomach-churning hunger. Instead, she sank against Kyle, her fingers curling into the padded gambeson he wore.

His mouth was hungry, skillful, his tongue plundering her mouth.

Eara groaned. She'd never been kissed like this. Ever. Her head swam, her knees went weak, and her legs would have given way entirely if he hadn't been holding her up.

Kyle gentled the kiss then, his hands sliding up to cup her face.

The shift caught Eara off-guard. One moment he'd been devouring her, the next he was savoring her as if she were a fine wine. She started to tremble as need ignited deep in her belly.

A man who could kiss like this was dangerous to a woman's sanity.

He turned her wits to porridge. Suddenly, she couldn't even remember what she'd been angry with him about. All fears of letting herself get close to anyone vanished. All she wanted was to taste him, to touch him.

Eventually, he ended their embrace. Hands sliding to Eara's shoulders, Kyle drew back, resting his forehead against hers for a long moment, as if gathering his own wits, before drawing back so that their gazes met.

Eara stared up at him, lips parted, desire pounding through her veins.

"I'm sorry, Eara," he rasped. "I shouldn't have done that."

"Aye, but ye did," she murmured huskily.

His green eyes guttered. "Do ye think me a beast?"

She swallowed. "No." It was the truth; all she wanted was for him to kiss her again, for him to set her body alight as no one else ever had.

He sucked in a deep breath before reaching up and stroking her cheek. He then caught a lock of her fine pale-blonde hair, wrapping it around his fingers. "Ye are so lovely, lass. When I first met ye, I thought ye were fragile … yet I soon learned that appearances deceive. Ye are tough, yet with a vulnerability ye try to hide." His throat bobbed then. "But I see it."

Silence fell while they stared at each other.

Part of Eara wanted to deny his words, to tell him he didn't know her at all. But he was right.

She *was* lonely. She *was* tired. Suddenly, she couldn't summon the strength to pretend otherwise. As much as she tried to deny it, there was something about Kyle MacAlister that made her feel safe.

"I want to be part of yer life," he continued, his voice roughening. "Aye, I'm not without faults … and I have three strong-willed daughters who will likely drive both of us mad … but my interest in ye is earnest. I'd rather drive a stake into my eye than hurt ye."

That was quite a statement, and for a few moments, Eara merely stared up at him. "I don't understand why ye'd want to live here with me," she murmured, finally finding her tongue. "Ye have a farmhouse of yer own, with plenty of space to accommodate a wife."

Kyle sighed. "That dwelling holds too many memories," he said with a shake of his head. "I plan to hand it over to my brother. He already runs the farm, so he might as well own it." He released her lock of hair, his thumb grazing her jawline instead. "It's time for a fresh start … for me and my girls."

Eara shivered at the heat and need his light touch roused. "And what about yer position as bailiff?" she asked, desperately trying to concentrate.

His lips lifted at the corners, even as his gaze remained intense. "A bailiff's time is largely his own. I'm busy during certain periods of the year and quiet at others. My work's ebb and flow would allow me to help my wife run her business."

Eara's heart did a little kick at these words. "God's blood," she murmured. "Ye really are in earnest about this?"

"I've never been more serious about anything, Eara." He paused then. "But what matters now is what *ye* want." Both his hands returned to her shoulders. "I'll admit, I delivered that proposal with all the grace of a sledgehammer … but rest assured, I'll not push ye into anything. If ye wish me gone, I shall leave ye be."

Silence fell once more, swelling between them. A nerve flickered in Kyle's cheek, yet he said nothing else.

Eara's pulse throbbed in her ears. This was it, the moment she had to make her choice. Fear was still there, dragging sharp claws down her back, but Kyle's hands held her firm.

She had to be honest with herself. What did she really want?

"I've had one or two proposals of marriage over the years," she admitted finally, her mouth curving just a little. "Yet that was most definitely the worst of them."

Kyle grimaced. "I was nervous."

Eara arched an eyebrow. "Ye were?" It was hard to believe the full-of-himself bailiff ever lacked confidence.

He swallowed. "Aye. Ye turn me into an awkward fool, Eara Mackay. I'll admit it. If ye hadn't yet realized … I'm besotted with ye."

Something melted inside her at these words, joy fluttering up. "Well, in that case, I should admit that ye turned my head a long while ago," she murmured as her hands slid up the hard wall of his chest. She felt the thunder of his heart under her right palm. Kyle wasn't lying; he *was* nervous. "And I've been fighting what I feel for ye ever since." She paused then, watching tenderness light in his expressive moss-green eyes. "I accept yer offer, Kyle. I shall be yer wife."

A smile flowered across his handsome face, his eyes crinkling at the corners. Kyle's breath gusted out of him as if he'd been holding it, waiting for her answer. "Ye will?" His voice held a faint note of insecurity as if he couldn't believe his ears.

The Mackay's bailiff wasn't as sure of himself as folk thought. He'd been ready for her to spurn him.

"Aye," she whispered.

"Ye won't regret it, lass." His hands cupped her face once more. "I swear I shall do all I can to ensure yer happiness."

The roughness of the callouses on his palms made Eara's breathing hitch. She wanted those hands on her naked skin, loving her, making her his. Her pulse started to race at the thought. Reaching up, she traced her fingers down his strong, bearded jaw and was rewarded by his sharp intake of breath.

His gaze hooded, and the air between them grew heavy with desire once more. "So," he said after a long pause. "When do I start?"

Eara inclined her head. "Start what?"

His green eyes twinkled. "Helping ye brew yer delicious ales, of course."

Eara laughed. She then went up on her toes, her lips grazing his. "All in good time, MacAlister," she murmured. "But right now, why don't ye kiss me again."

The End

HEART OF ICE

A REBELLIOUS HIGHLAND HEARTS SHORT STORY

*Dun Ugadale,
Kintyre Peninsula, Scotland*

Yuletide, 1454

SHEENA STOOD AT the window, watching the snowflakes flutter down.

She wasn't fond of winter, especially now that she was older, yet she had always been entranced by the beauty of falling snow. The flakes were delicate, gentle, and silent as they drifted through the gelid air and kissed the ground.

Watching the wintry scene soothed her and eased the nagging sense of passing time.

Another Yuletide had arrived.

Another year had passed.

She was getting older; they all were.

Alone in the ladies' solar, Sheena pulled the fur stole she wore tighter around her shoulders. A fire blazed in the hearth just a few yards away, yet she'd rolled up the sacking at the window so she could watch the snow. The damp cold drilled into her bones, but she remained where she was.

It was mid-afternoon, and usually the other women would join her at this hour. However, with Yule approaching, Rose and Davina were helping Cory and his assistants bake honey cakes, studded with dried plums. Meanwhile, Bonnie, who was heavy with bairn these days, was taking an afternoon nap.

Sheena didn't mind her own company; actually, there were times when she preferred it.

The happy chatter of her daughters-by-marriage sometimes grew wearying. She was sure they thought her a bitter old shrew, yet none of them had lived in her shoes.

They hadn't suffered her disappointments.

As Sheena continued to gaze out the window, a figure emerged from the smith's forge into the snow-covered barmkin below.

Despite that it was cold enough to freeze the breath, her stepson wore nothing but soot-covered braies and a sleeveless leather vest. Brodie's brawny arms gleamed with sweat as he trudged through the snow, bucket in one hand and hammer in the other. Reaching the water trough near the well, he broke the ice with a couple of smacks of his hammer before plunging the wooden pail into the water.

Sheena's mouth pursed as she watched him.

She hadn't caught more than a few glimpses of Brodie since his return from the north around four months earlier—since his disgrace. After running off to pursue a woman far above his rank and then abducting her, he'd nearly caused a feud to erupt between the Mackays and the Forbeses. Fortunately, Iver had prevented him, yet the incident had driven a wedge between the brothers, and Brodie kept to his forge these days. He hadn't ventured inside the broch once since his return.

His absence didn't bother Sheena. She and Brodie had been enemies for years, yet at the same time, catching the odd glimpse of him, as she did now, gave her a strange pang. Her chest constricted, and her belly clenched.

What was it? Guilt … regret? She wasn't sure.

Ye are growing daft in yer old age, she murmured to herself. Aye, that must be it, for there had been a time when merely the sight of Brodie—constant proof of her husband's indiscretions—made her blood boil.

These past few months though, her feelings toward her stepson were more … complicated. He'd suffered a tragedy, and she couldn't find it in her heart to rejoice over it.

Pushing aside the uncomfortable sensations, Sheena watched Brodie disappear inside the maw of the forge once more. Moments later, the rhythmic clang of a hammer on metal echoed out into the barmkin.

She shivered then, as the cold finally became too much, and was about to step back from the window and pull down the sacking, when a horn blew.

Sheena stilled, her gaze shifting to where two of Kerr's men, huddled under heavy woolen cloaks, hurried from the gatehouse and started winching up the portcullis. Kerr himself walked out into the snow, sinking up to his ankles with each stride.

With his hood pushed back, his shoulder-length ice-blond hair bright despite the snowy day, the sight of her youngest son made Sheena's mouth soften into a half-smile. Although she rarely showed Iver, Lennox, and Kerr affection—for it wasn't her way—Sheena's three sons were her world. Aye, they'd frustrated her at times over the years. However, what mother didn't gnash her teeth at the foolhardy decisions of her sons?

The portcullis rumbled up, and then a few moments later, men on horseback rode into the barmkin.

The man leading them wore a sash of muted green and blue. Big, bearded, and broad-shouldered, with a wild mane of black hair threaded with silver, she recognized him instantly.

Despite herself, Sheena's mouth kicked up at the corners, warmth flickering to life deep in her chest.

She couldn't believe it. Was she actually pleased to see this man?

She truly was going soft in the head, if she was. Colin Campbell aggravated her immensely at times, and he made a beeline for her whenever he visited.

As if feeling someone's gaze upon him, the Lord of Glenorchy glanced up, his attention fixing upon the window where she stood.

A heartbeat later, a roguish grin split Colin's face.

Swallowing her smile, Sheena raised a hand in acknowledgment.

Colin was loud, brash, and talked too much. His daughter was wed to her son Lennox, and he was a regular visitor to Dun Ugadale. Sheena had known he was coming yet was surprised—and more than a little discomforted—by her reaction to Colin's arrival.

Ye have gone and done it now, she chastised herself as she stepped back from the window and yanked the sacking down. *Now the man will stick to ye like a bur for the rest of the festive season.*

"Ye are looking well, Sheena."

With a sigh, Sheena glanced up from where she'd been cutting into a piece of venison on her trencher.

Colin Campbell met her eye, bold as ever. His mouth had curved into an appreciative smile.

"Am I?" she replied lightly. When Campbell had started complimenting her on his first visits to Dun Ugadale, she'd cut him off at the knees. However, these days, she let him flatter her—just as long as he didn't push it too far.

"Aye." His smile widened. "The firelight gilds yer hair and skin … and darkens yer eyes."

Sheena huffed a laugh. She then glanced down at the goblet of wine at his elbow. "How many of them have ye downed, Colin?"

"This is my first."

She cocked an eyebrow, making it clear she didn't believe him. Observing Colin then, she noted that he too was looking well. He'd been taking care of himself better of late. His cheeks had lost their high color, as if he was drinking more moderately, and he'd lost weight off his belly. He'd also trimmed his beard. When she'd first met him, it had been as wild as his hair, yet it was neat now, emphasizing the chiseled strength of his jaw.

He was around ten years her junior and still an attractive man.

"I'm sure ye have had plenty of men tell ye of yer loveliness over the years," he continued, ignoring her incredulous look. "Ye must surely tire of it?"

"I might have received a few compliments in my youth," she replied archly. "But those days have long gone."

Her supper companion snorted, dismissing her comment with a wave of his large hand.

The pair of them sat at one end of the chieftain's table in Dun Ugadale's hall.

A heavy pall of peat smoke hung under the rafters. The acrid smell caught in the back of Sheena's throat, as did the odor of wet wool, leather, and stale sweat. Fortunately, other more pleasant smells did their best to counteract the disagreeable ones. The aroma of roast venison, fresh bread, and pine.

Yule was just a night away, and Rose and Davina—under Bonnie's guidance—had decorated the hall beautifully. Ivy festooned the smoke-blackened rafters, as did wreaths of holly. Banks of candles lined the tables, nestled amongst sprigs of fragrant-scented pine.

Colin picked up a ewer of bramble wine then and topped up both their goblets. "What a fine feast yer cooks put on … I always eat and drink well here."

Sheena cut him an arch look. "So, that's why ye visit Dun Ugadale so often, is it?"

Colin's expression sobered then. "I enjoy seeing my daughter, of course." Both their gazes shifted across the table, to where Davina was laughing at something Lennox had just said. "It gladdens my heart to see her so happy."

Indeed, Davina glowed these days, her earlier fragility a thing of the past. There was a bloom to her cheeks, a gleam to her eye, that had been missing when she'd first arrived at Dun Ugdale. And despite that she was four months with bairn now, she hadn't suffered from any sickness as yet.

Colin glanced back at Sheena, his mouth quirking. "Davina isn't the only person I look forward to seeing though." His grey-blue eyes darkened then. "Ye are worthy of traveling days for too."

Despite herself, Sheena found her lips curving. "Ye are a silver-tongued rogue," she replied. Picking up the goblet, she took a sip of bramble wine. It was rich and spicy, a Yuletide treat. "I wouldn't be surprised if ye've slayed more than a few women with that charm ye wield."

Colin gave a low, rumbling laugh.

Warmth filtered over Sheena. She liked his laugh. It was earthy and a little rough, much like the man himself.

"Aye, I liked the lasses in my day," he admitted with a wink. "My wife said I could have charmed the devil himself." His expression softened then, with a hint of wistfulness as memories caught him up. "Aileen always appreciated a compliment."

Sheena pulled a face. "Men," she muttered. "Ye always think flattery will win a woman over." She paused then before adding. "My husband was charming enough in his day as well."

Colin met her eye then, his head inclining. "That's the first time ye have ever mentioned Reid Mackay to me."

Sheena grimaced and took another sip of wine. "Aye, well, there are plenty of good reasons for that … as ye well know."

"Many years have passed since he left this world," Colin pointed out gently. "Do ye still bear him ill will?"

In the past, Sheena would have turned on anyone who asked such a bold question, yet she didn't now. Colin was right. Time had moved on. Reid had been dead a long while, yet even the steady march of the years couldn't heal some wounds.

She didn't bear *Brodie* the same ill will these days, as she had when he was a bairn, but she couldn't think about her dead husband without her mouth souring.

"I do," she admitted, her voice roughening just a little. She glanced away then so he wouldn't see the sudden vulnerability in her eyes.

"Why?"

Sheena's mouth pursed. Lord, the bramble wine must be strong if she was being so frank with Colin. Usually, she let him do all the talking when they sat in the hall together. Yet, this eve, the man was full of questions.

"Ye know what he did to me," she replied, her tone sharpening. "Do ye think I could ever forgive and forget?"

"Ye might."

Sheena cut Colin an irritated look, to find him watching her steadily. "Bitterness is a poison, Sheena," he said softly. "I too have sucked from its teat ... resentment left to fester robs ye of joy."

"Maybe," she replied, her tone chilling now. She'd had enough of Colin Campbell's probing. It was time to end this exchange. "But the choice is mine, is it not?"

His gaze never left hers as he slowly nodded. "It is."

A cry echoed down the table then, intruding upon their conversation.

Sheena's attention flew to where Bonnie sat next to Iver. Heavy with bairn, her belly so huge that she had to sit a foot back from the table, the laird's wife had doubled over. Bonnie's lovely face was strained, her bright blue eyes wide.

"Mo chridhe." Iver had turned to her, brow furrowing, his gaze alarmed. "Is it time?"

Bonnie nodded. "I've no idea what to expect," she gasped. "But … I think so."

Iver shoved back his carven wooden chair and scooped his wife carefully up in his arms. He then glanced over at where Kerr had already gotten to his feet. "Fetch the midwife!"

The midwife arrived and took up her place at Bonnie's side in the bedchamber. Sheena, Rose, and Davina assisted where they could, bringing in basins of hot water and clean cloths, ready for the birth—but they were wary of getting underfoot.

Unfortunately, right from the beginning, Bonnie struggled.

Sheena had brought three babes out successfully into the world and knew how painful it was. Iver had been the hardest to birth, and since he'd been her first, she'd also been frightened. She saw the same fear in Bonnie's eyes now as she bore down with each birthing pain.

Beathas, the midwife, was an experienced and no-nonsense woman, yet Sheena watched her closely.

And as the hours slowly inched by, and evening became night, Beathas's long face grew tense, her brown eyes worried.

"Something is amiss, isn't it?" Sheena finally asked.

They'd reached the early hours of the morning now. Davina was dozing in a chair in the corner of the chamber while Rose and Sheena sat on stools next to the bed.

Beathas nodded, a muscle in her jaw feathering. "The birth isn't progressing," she murmured. "I will need assistance, I fear."

"Why isn't the bairn coming?" Bonnie panted. Sweat slicked her face, and her red hair was now plastered to her scalp. She was breathing hard, eyes glassy.

"I believe the babe is positioned wrongly," Beathas replied gently. "I shall need help to birth it."

Sheena rose to her feet. "I will send a rider out to Ceann Locha … to fetch the healer," she announced, even as a sickening sensation clutched at her belly.

Childbirth was such a dangerous time for women. Death always waited close by, like a carrion crow waiting to swoop.

Emerging from the chamber, Sheena found Iver pacing the hallway outside. His face was pale, his eyes bloodshot with tiredness and worry.

"The birth is taking longer than it should," she informed him, deciding it was best to be direct about these things. "Beathas wishes for the healer from Ceann Locha to attend." She paused then, watching his dark-blue eyes gutter. "Malcolm is skilled indeed … he will be able to help. I will organize for a rider to go now."

They stared at each other a moment, and then Sheena stepped forward, placing a hand on her son's arm. "She's fighting, Iver … and we shall do all we can to help her." Her voice was low yet fierce. Her son needed her strength right now.

Iver nodded, reaching up and placing a hand over hers. "Thank ye, Ma." His voice was rough, strained, yet he was keeping himself together.

Sheena left him then, picking up her skirts and making her way off the landing and down the spiral stone stairwell.

She'd just reached the ground floor, and was crossing to the door that would lead her out of the broch, when a tall, broad-shouldered figure approached.

The rest of the broch was slumbering, yet Colin Campbell had been sitting on a stool by the hearth. "What news?" he greeted her, his brow furrowed with concern.

"The birth isn't going well," she told him, her throat constricting.

Lord, she'd held on earlier, yet there was something about Campbell's solid presence that made her want to crumble against him.

Inwardly berating herself, she gulped down a lungful of air. "I'm going to find a rider to fetch the healer from Ceann Locha."

"No need," Colin replied with a shake of his head. "I shall go."

Sheena frowned. "Are ye sure? It's a freezing night … I don't want to—"

The Lord of Glenorchy flashed her a careless smile as he made for the door. He then grabbed his heavy fur mantle that hung on a peg next to it. "Don't worry about me … I've ridden in worse weather than this."

Sheena's lips parted as she readied herself to argue with him, to point out that he was pigheaded and too old to go off on such a ride. However, it was too late.

Colin Campbell had already departed.

Colin returned with Malcolm the healer, just as the first glow of dawn lightened the eastern sky.

Bonnie still hadn't given birth, and Iver was growing frantic.

Even Sheena's increasingly faltering words of reassurance couldn't ease the panic that rippled across his face with every raw cry that echoed from the chamber.

Both Colin and Malcolm were sweat-soaked and dusted in snow. Neither man said a word as the healer let himself into the birthing chamber, while Colin remained out on the landing with Iver and Sheena. However, when Colin's blue-grey gaze met hers, it was full of questions.

He wanted to know how things were progressing.

Swallowing hard, Sheena gave a shake of her head.

Beyond the door, Bonnie's cries were gradually getting weaker. She'd been toiling all night now—and wouldn't be able to go on much longer.

Malcolm had to be able to help her.

Outside on the landing, the three of them remained silent.

A moment later, an anguished cry filtered through the door.

Iver murmured an oath and stepped forward, placing his hands on the thick oak that provided a barrier between him and his wife. Eyes fluttering shut, he then leaned forward, resting his forehead on the door. It was cruel indeed that men were not allowed inside a birthing chamber. Midwives complained that they got in the way during the birth, and some husbands couldn't withstand the stress and fainted.

"I can't stand it," he whispered hoarsely. "I want to help her … but I can't." His shoulders heaved as another cry of agony followed. "Christ's bones, I've never felt so useless in my life."

Colin stepped up and placed a steadying hand on Iver's shoulder. Usually, the Lord of Glenorchy had something to say, yet not this morning. Instead, he just offered Iver silent support.

Likewise, Sheena held her tongue. What could she say to make things better? Bonnie had been struggling for a long while now—too long.

Footfalls approached then from below. Lennox and Kerr appeared on the stairs, their faces solemn. Sheena cut them both a warning look as they ascended the steps. They all needed to remain calm and quiet at present; Iver needed their strength.

It was hushed for a short while on the other side of the door. After a spell, Sheena caught the low, reassuring rumble of Malcolm's voice. And then the cries began once more.

Sheena clenched her hands by her sides, so hard that her fingernails dug into her skin.

Please Lord, she silently prayed. *Spare Bonnie and her bairn.* Her heart started to gallop then as she recalled how harsh she'd been with her daughter-by-marriage when she'd first arrived at Dun Ugadale. She'd flayed Bonnie with her tongue and taken pleasure in telling the lass who her father was, in shaming her.

Shame prickled over Sheena as the memories assaulted her.

Aye, Iver had forced her to apologize to Bonnie afterward, yet she hadn't truly been sorry. She'd just swallowed her resentment and tried to move on. But with the passing of the months, she'd grown fond of her daughter-by-marriage.

How could anyone fail to love someone like Bonnie? She was gentle-natured, a kind soul who cared deeply for others.

Her decency made Sheena feel like a miserable wretch.

Campbell was right. Resentment was a venom—and it did sap all the joy from life.

Tears filled her eyes then, her vision blurring.

Let her live, she silently begged. *Dear Lord, I swear I shall give Bonnie a proper apology this time, a heartfelt one ... I will be a nicer person from this day forth.*

But the cries went on and on, and with each one, Sheena felt as if someone were ripping out her innards.

Iver still braced himself against the door, eyes squeezed shut. His strong body trembled as he held in his fear, his anguish.

Stepping forward, Sheena took hold of his arm, gripping it firmly.

Iver opened his eyes, his tortured gaze shifting to her. Sheena stared back, all the love she felt in her heart pouring out of her. She wouldn't tell him everything would be all right, for she had no way of knowing. All the same, he would know that she cared deeply about what happened to Bonnie and her bairn.

Her heart wasn't made of ice, after all.

The cries inside the birthing chamber grew louder then, rising to a sharp scream.

And then, the noise cut off.

Iver breathed a curse and grabbed the door handle. He'd reached his limit and wouldn't be parted from his beloved Bonnie any longer.

However, before he could open the door, another wail filtered through.

This one wasn't the cry of an exhausted woman in pain, but the lusty cry of a newborn.

Iver heaved a sob, while Sheena's legs went weak with relief.

She staggered, and suddenly a strong arm was there, supporting her. She looked up into Colin Campbell's blue-grey eyes, to find him grinning down at her. "Well, that's a bonnie sound if ever I heard one."

It was crowded in the birthing chamber, yet no one seemed to notice or care. Iver, Colin, Sheena, Lennox, and Kerr all pushed inside to find Bonnie propped up on a nest of pillows. The midwife held a small squalling infant in her arms, while the healer cut the umbilical cord with a sharp knife. Rose and Davina, their faces slack with exhaustion, sat at the head of the bed, flanking Bonnie.

"Ye have a son, Mackay," Malcolm greeted Iver, flashing him a relieved smile.

Tears trickled down Iver's face as he approached the bed. His gaze alighted on the tiny new life that Beathas now wrapped in a linen shawl, his lips parting with wonder. Yet an instant later, his attention shifted to his wife. "Ye did well, mo chridhe," he said huskily. "Ye have been so brave."

Bonnie gave a sob. "It was so hard … I didn't think I'd manage."

"The bairn came out feet first," the midwife informed them. "I couldn't have birthed him without Malcolm's help."

Iver met the healer's gaze then, a long look passing between them.

The laird would never forget what Malcolm had done here.

Rose moved aside so Iver could sink onto the stool next to Bonnie. Tenderly taking his wife's hand, Iver leaned in and kissed her. He then shot another look at the healer, this one concerned. "Is she harmed?"

"The birth was a hard one," Malcolm replied, his expression sobering. "I must keep an eye on her … for the bleeding hasn't yet stopped."

Standing at the foot of the bed, Sheena's gaze fell to the blood-stained sheets. Her belly dropped then. There was *a lot* of blood.

"Bonnie must also pass the afterbirth," Beathas added. Her face was now grave.

It seemed that Bonnie wasn't out of the woods yet, and the joy inside the chamber dimmed just a little.

"Don't fash yerself, Iver," Bonnie said, breaking the awkward silence. Her voice was weak, her face as pale as milk, yet her eyes shone. "All will be well."

Sheena's chest constricted, even as her attention returned to the crimson stain upon the bed. It wasn't just the birthing of a bairn that put a woman at risk, but the time swiftly following. Sheena's younger sister had died after having her third bairn; she'd bled out afterward.

They would have to watch Bonnie carefully in the coming hours.

This Yuletide was much quieter than most. A great oaken log burned in the hearth in the hall, and the aroma of roasting meats, pastry, and cakes drifted through the broch and out into the barmkin beyond.

Yet there wouldn't be a Yuletide feast at noon as planned. Most of their family members retired to their chambers, to rest, but Iver remained with Bonnie, as did Sheena. Together, they nervously waited to see her rally.

As noon approached, Sheena went down to the kitchen and retrieved three cups of hot caudle and a platter of honey cakes studded with dried plums. She then carried them upstairs.

The midwife had long departed, but Malcolm remained. The healer's face was drawn with fatigue, although relief flickered across his face when Sheena passed him a cup of caudle and a cake.

"Caudle will be just the thing for Bonnie," he said approvingly.

Sheena nodded. The rich mix of cream, egg yolks, honey, and oats was a fortifying drink indeed. Ideal for a woman who'd recently given birth.

Iver flashed his mother a grateful smile as he took the two other cups and handed one to Bonnie.

"Thank ye, Sheena," Bonnie said softly. "That's very kind."

"How are ye feeling?" Sheena asked, pulling up a stool on the opposite side to Iver.

"Well enough." Bonnie managed a wan smile. "Just exhausted."

The bairn slept against her breast, and something tugged deep in Sheena's chest as she viewed his crumpled wee face. He was so small, so vulnerable. "Has he a name yet?"

"Aye … Reid," Bonnie replied, her gaze meeting Sheena's. "Are ye happy with that?"

Sheena's breathing hitched. Of course, it made sense that Iver would wish his firstborn to be named after his father. Despite the fact he'd strayed from the marital bed, Reid Mackay had been a good man. Even so, Bonnie understood why Sheena might be upset.

Her gentle concern for others—even when her own situation was of more importance—made Sheena's throat thicken. Reaching out, she placed a hand on Bonnie's arm. "Aye, lass," she murmured. "It's an excellent name."

Next to Bonnie, Iver's eyes widened. No doubt, he'd been ready for a fight.

However, he wasn't going to get one.

Silence fell then, while Sheena focused her attention on Bonnie once more. She'd wanted to apologize to her daughter-by-marriage when they were alone, yet that wouldn't be possible.

And she wouldn't wait. Bonnie needed to hear these words now.

"I am truly sorry, lass," she murmured. "For the way I treated ye when ye first came here." Pausing, Sheena sucked in a fortifying breath before plowing on. "Ye are the best thing that ever happened to Iver. Ye have made him so happy … and ye have brought such joy to this broch. I should have told ye earlier how much ye mean to me" —Sheena's voice wobbled as emotion threatened to overtake her— "And ye do … ye are the sweet-natured daughter I always wanted, yet never deserved."

Bonnie stared back at Sheena, her lips parting in surprise.

Indeed, both Iver and Malcolm were watching her as if she'd just sprouted whiskers.

Sheena didn't blame them. Her behavior was altogether out of character. Nonetheless, something had changed in her of late.

Ironically, Brodie was the cause. Catching glimpses of his unhappy face in the barmkin over the past months, she'd found herself reflecting on the past, and questioning her own choices. He didn't deserve the scorn she'd heaped on him. No one did.

The hard shell Sheena presented to the world had started to crack, and then Bonnie's difficult birth had caused it to shatter.

She didn't want to be that woman any longer.

Bonnie was still weak and vulnerable; she was still at risk after giving birth. Sheena couldn't bear the thought of letting another moment pass without speaking plainly.

"I know I appear pitiless at times," Sheena admitted after a lengthy pause. "Yet I'm not without a heart."

Bonnie's bright blue eyes glittered with tears as she stared back. And then, she handed Iver her cup of caudle and reached out, catching Sheena's hand in hers. "I know," she whispered.

"Here's to Reid Mackay!" Lennox held his goblet of wine aloft, a wide smile upon his face. "And to his courageous mother. Good health to them both!"

"Aye!" The answering chorus rose high into the rafters of the hall.

Sheena too lifted her goblet in a toast to the newborn bairn and Bonnie. She felt almost giddy with relief this evening.

Many hours had passed since the birth, and the healer was now satisfied that Bonnie was no longer in immediate danger. She was weak and sore and would need a few days to recover—but the worst was over.

As Bonnie couldn't join them for the Yule celebrations, Iver had remained with his wife upstairs while one of Cory's lads brought up food for them. However, the rest of the family, and the Mackay retainers, gathered in the hall for a magnificent belated Yuletide feast.

Taking a sip of bramble wine, Sheena let her gaze travel over the long table that groaned under the weight of the dishes placed there. The centerpiece was a spit-roasted suckling pig that had been stuffed with chestnut and apple. There were many other special dishes too: grouse pies with rich suet pastry, venison stew, roasted fowl, fragrant honey cakes, and custards sweetened with honey.

"Cory has outdone himself," Kerr announced from farther down the table. "I swear this is his best spread yet."

Beside Sheena, Colin Campbell snorted. "I really should steal yer cook for a few months ... and get him to teach mine a few tricks."

Sheena eyed him. "I don't think we could ever spare Cory," she pointed out.

"Too right," Kerr agreed as he helped himself to a large wedge of pie. "Ye'd have to send yer cook here."

"I just might," Colin replied.

The feasting began, and for a while, conversation settled. Sheena, too, ate with relish. Earlier in the day, she'd felt sick to her stomach with worry over Bonnie, yet now she could relax a little.

"Ye are a grandmother now, Sheena," Colin said then as he refilled her wine. "What do ye think about that?"

She favored him with an arch look. "It makes me feel old."

He winked before indicating to Davina. "Aye, well … I'll soon be a grand Da." Colin's eyes twinkled as he exchanged a smile with his daughter.

Warmth bloomed under Sheena's ribcage as she viewed the affection between them. "And ye will make a fine one, I'm sure," she murmured.

Sheena didn't think she'd ever be the sort of grandmother who fussed over bairns—most likely her grandbairns would be scared of her—yet she could see that Colin would be different. He'd likely bounce the children on his knee and tickle them until they squealed. There was a warmth to him, one that she'd grown to appreciate.

The truth was that there were many things about the Lord of Glenorchy that she'd grown to like. His strength. His directness. And his big heart.

Colin's gaze shifted to her then, and his smile changed.

It became more intimate, as if he'd read her thoughts and wished her to know so.

Heat flushed over Sheena. She wasn't her usual prickly self this evening; her defenses were down.

What was she doing entertaining such thoughts?

She was a grandmother now—an *old* woman.

Flustered, she tore her gaze from Colin's and tried to focus on her meal. Yet, for the remainder of it, she was acutely aware of his presence at her side.

Drawing her cloak close, Sheena walked across the barmkin toward the gate. Her boots crunched over fresh snow, and the gelid air bit at her skin, yet today, she welcomed the cold.

After days cooped up inside the broch, she longed to get out for a walk.

It was a quiet, still morning, save for the rhythmic clang of metal drifting out from the forge. Sheena's gaze narrowed as she peered at the open doorway. She could just make out her stepson's heavily muscled form as he hammered.

Brodie hadn't seen her, and she wouldn't interrupt him.

What would she say anyway? Apologize for everything? She'd be there all day.

Even so, her step slowed.

She'd resented Brodie since his birth, as she had his mother—the cook who'd stolen her husband's affections—but there was no denying she'd been unfair to him all these years. They weren't related by blood, and yet Brodie carried a similar affliction to her. He held onto things for far too long and let the past embitter him.

Nonetheless, the pair of them would never be friends, and she knew her stepson resented her deeply. He wouldn't welcome a visit from her.

And so, Sheena kept walking, out of the broch and down the causeway that led into the village below.

Bairns played in the snow. They lobbed snowballs at each other, their shrieks carrying high into the pale sky.

Sheena's mouth lifted at the corners. To be so young and full of life. Those days were far behind her now.

This morning, she felt as if her youth was nothing but a distant memory. How she wished she'd cherished it more. How she wished she hadn't held onto things. Bonnie wasn't like her. Nor was Davina or Rose. All three of her daughters-by-marriage rode with life rather than fighting it.

Deep in thought, Sheena continued walking through the village and up onto the hill beyond. This was where they had the Beltaine and Samhuinn bonfires. It was a lovely spot, one that afforded her a view of the broch, rising up from its rocky pinnacle, and the rolling snow-clad hills beyond.

Sheena reached the top, yet instead of lingering to admire the view, she decided to walk a little farther. Full of restless energy this morning, she felt disquieted and needed to burn off the unsettling sensation.

She was moving on when a male voice hailed her.

"Sheena!"

Halting, she glanced over her shoulder to see a burly figure with wild dark hair, trudging up the slope after her.

Colin Campbell approached.

"God's troth, woman … ye march like a warrior on parade," he huffed, reaching her side at the top of the hill.

"Aye, well … I don't like to waste time," Sheena replied, flashing him a rueful smile. "Were ye trying to catch me up?"

He nodded. Colin's gaze roamed over her face then, uncertainty flashing in his eyes. "Are ye not wanting company?"

Sheena sighed. There would have been a time when she'd have snarled at anyone who intruded upon her solitude—especially Colin Campbell. On his first visits to Dun Ugadale, the man had irritated her no end. But he'd grown on her of late, and when she'd seen him approach, the same warmth that both pleased and discomforted her had blossomed under her breastbone.

"I find that yer company isn't too odious," she admitted, her mouth curving. "Indeed, I must admit that ye are actually growing on me."

Colin flashed her a grin at this. In the pale winter light, she could see the signs of age upon him, the crow's feet at the corners of his eyes and the silver lacing his dark hair and beard. But she was sure every line on her own face would be highlighted similarly.

Sheena's breathing grew shallow. Colin had a smile that lit up his face, and now that he'd trimmed his beard so that it framed his strong jawline, she noted his cheek dimpled when he grinned or laughed. His grey-blue eyes were bright, sharp, and filled with good humor. They also saw her as no one else did.

Her belly fluttered.

Mother Mary, there was no denying it. She *was* attracted to him. She had been for a while now—that was why she hadn't clawed him to shreds when he continued to seek out her company.

Stepping close, Colin raised a hand, pushing a lock of hair off her face. "Ye are wearing yer hair unbound," he murmured. "I like it."

The excitement in her stomach twisted harder, and suddenly her chest rose and fell sharply. Sheena usually wore her hair knotted into a severe bun at the base of her neck or braided tightly around the crown of her head. The fact she'd wandered outdoors with her silver mane in disarray showed that she wasn't herself this morning.

Her gaze traveled over his face then, focusing on his mouth. Colin had beautifully-molded, sensual lips. Why hadn't she ever noticed that before?

Marking the direction of her gaze, that mouth tilted into an arrogant, purely-male smile, and then he was leaning in, brushing his lips across hers.

Sheena froze.

It had been a long while since she'd been kissed—so long, in fact, that she couldn't remember the last time. In truth, she'd never thought to be embraced ever again.

As such, the rush of heat that surged over her when his mouth brushed hers once more took Sheena by surprise. She gasped, her lips parting, and Colin deepened the kiss. Stepping close, he slid his hands through her hair, cradling the back of her head as his tongue explored her mouth with slow, deliberate sensuality.

Need started to pulse low in Sheena's belly.

Lord, what was this?

It was as if he'd just woken her body from a long sleep. He tasted faintly of the watered-down ale he'd drunk to break his fast and smelled of smoke and leather.

Sheena's pulse started to thud against her breastbone.

This was delicious. Perhaps Reid had once kissed her like this, years ago, before their love turned to ashes—but so many years had passed she couldn't remember.

All she could focus on was the way Colin's mouth mated with hers and the deep, sensual promise of it.

For a few moments, she forgot she was now a grandmother, a woman far past her prime in life. Suddenly, she was ageless.

Her hands lifted, sliding over the quilted gambeson he wore under his fur cloak. And as she slid her palms over the breadth of his chest, she felt the thunder of his heart.

A heady sense of power thrilled through her veins. Colin might be acting as if he kissed women like this regularly, yet this was affecting him as strongly as it was her.

Sheena stroked her tongue against his, excitement quickening further as he groaned. A moment later, she gently nipped his lower lip.

Breathing hard, Colin drew back. His eyes were hooded with lust, his expression hungry. He placed his hands on her shoulders then, staring down at her. "We'd better stop there," he said, a rasp to his voice. "Or I might just throw ye down in the snow and take ye right here."

Sheena's breathing caught.

She might have forgotten what it was like to be kissed by her husband, but never in all their years of marriage had Reid ever said anything so lusty to her.

A restless ache started to pulse between her thighs. There was a part of her—a reckless side she'd never known she possessed—that wished to push him, to see if he'd make good on his threat.

Nonetheless, she reined the impulse in.

Moments passed, and then reality intruded upon the cocoon of lust the pair of them had woven.

Sheena murmured an oath. "I don't know what's come over me," she muttered. "I must be sickening."

Colin huffed a soft laugh. "Well, I know *I* am." One of his hands lifted from her shoulder, and he traced his knuckles gently along her jawline. "I'm pining for *ye*, Sheena."

Her heart kicked hard.

His mouth quirked. "Aye, ye heard me right. I'm like a lad who has lost his wits over a lass for the first time." He paused then, his gaze fusing with hers. "Why do ye think I visit so often … or seek ye out every time I do?"

Sheena stared back at him, speechless. Of course, she'd realized Colin Campbell liked her. But it had never dawned on her that it might run deeper.

"I want to marry ye … to spend the rest of my days at yer side," he declared then, his voice roughening. "Will ye do me the honor of becoming my wife?"

Sheena's breathing hitched, and when she finally answered, her voice came out strangled. "But why would ye shackle yerself to me? Ye could choose a young wife … ye could have more bairns … another family."

"I don't want any of that. I want ye."

"But I'm *old*." Panic started to beat in her chest like a caged bird. "I have eight and fifty winters … God's teeth, I'm at least a decade yer senior."

"Nine years actually," he replied, his mouth curving. His other hand raised, and he gently cupped her face. "But it matters not. Ye wear yer years with dignity … ye are still the rarest beauty I have ever seen." His gaze lowered to her lips. "And yer mouth is sweeter than anything I've tasted."

Sheena sighed, her eyes fluttering shut as longing rose like a tide within her. "Lord help me, how am I supposed to resist when ye say things like that?"

Colin gave a low, rumbling laugh. "Don't then. Say 'aye' to my offer of marriage, and make me the happiest man in Scotland."

Warmth suffused Sheena then as if she'd just lowered herself into a delicious steaming bath. Suddenly, she couldn't think of any good reason why she should deny him, or her. Opening her eyes, she met his gaze. Colin stared down at her, his expression hopeful, vulnerable.

It would be so easy to crush him right now, yet she never would. This man had just handed her his heart, and she would protect it, cherish it.

Offering him a slow smile, even as his pulse went wild underneath her palm, Sheena whispered her answer. "Aye."

The End

HEART OF FIRE

A REBELLIOUS HIGHLAND HEARTS SHORT STORY

The Cairngorms
The Scottish Highlands

Summer, 1454

THE MAN DREW her attention far too often—and she wanted to hate him for it.

But she didn't, and that was the problem.

Curse her, why couldn't she?

Seated astride her garron as they traveled down a deep, wide glen, Inghinn glared at Captain Errol's broad back. As always, the warrior rode with calm self-assurance, his gaze sweeping their surroundings. Like her, Errol had served the clan-chief for many years—a silent, watchful presence.

They were journeying through a wild, sparsely inhabited area, and as such, he was on the alert for outlaws. The remoteness of the Cairngorms made it an ideal choice for those looking to prey on travelers. Errol couldn't afford to let his attention slip, especially since he was escorting the Forbes himself, and his daughter, home.

Tearing her attention from Errol, Inghinn glanced over her shoulder at where Greer Forbes rode behind her upon a prancing grey palfrey. Usually, Lady Greer wore a smile upon her lovely face, her grey eyes sparkling with life. But this afternoon, there was a dullness to her. Even her wheat-colored hair, which shone even on the greyest day, seemed lifeless.

At least her eyes were no longer puffy and bloodshot from weeping through the night. In the past days, Greer had rallied. She was a strong lass, tougher than most folk gave her credit for. Nonetheless, Greer had been suffering. They'd left Dun Ugadale on the Kintyre Peninsula just a week earlier, and for the first few nights, Inghinn had lain awake on her sheepskin, listening to the muffled sound of her mistress's weeping. It was a knife to the heart to hear her so upset.

Inghinn had been Lady Greer's maid since the lass's tenth birthday. She'd been young herself then, just twenty winters, and had watched Greer grow from a happy, lively bairn into an equally sunny-natured young woman. Inghinn loved her with as much fierceness as if they were kin, yet despite that they'd always shared an easy relationship, she was careful not to overstep the invisible lines of rank that separated them.

As such, she'd watched the lady's misery and held her tongue.

If Greer wished to talk to her about the man she'd clearly fallen in love with, she would.

Inghinn's gaze roamed over Greer's pale, strained face for a moment, disquiet flickering through her. She'd known, from the moment she'd seen Greer and Brodie's gazes lock in the barmkin of Dun Ugadale broch, on the day of their arrival, that her young mistress was about to learn one of life's cruel lessons.

That a man could tear a woman's heart to pieces if she didn't guard it.

Stifling a sigh, Inghinn turned back to the direction of travel.

She wished it wasn't so, but in her experience, love meant pain.

Love meant humiliation.

Lost in bitter memories that she hated dwelling on, yet sometimes couldn't prevent herself from torturing herself with, Inghinn glanced over at the sweeping granite peak of Ben Macdui, the highest of the mountains within the Cairngorms. Outlined against purple storm clouds, it was stoic, sculpted, and it made her feel very small and alone in the world.

Moments passed, and then the fine hair on the back of her neck prickled, drawing her out of her brooding.

Someone was watching her.

Tensing, she cut her gaze sideways. With a jolt, she realized that Errol had slowed his courser so that he now rode alongside Crabapple.

His dark gaze bored into her.

Inghinn started to sweat. Even so, she rose to the challenge—as she always did. Her chin lifted, and she frowned. Errol Forbes wouldn't humiliate her ever again. She'd made herself that promise nearly a decade earlier, and she reminded herself of it again now.

Don't let him intimidate ye.

Usually, their staring contests were conducted in silence. Ever since that fateful night, only a handful of cold words had passed between them. As such, Errol surprised her now by speaking.

"I'd watch yerself, Inghinn," he drawled, his voice a low rumble. "If the wind changes, that furrow upon yer brow will remain forever."

Heat fired under Inghinn's ribs. She couldn't believe he'd summoned the nerve to talk to her. At Druminnor, it had been easy enough to avoid each other. However, on this trip, they'd been thrown together. The only thing that made it bearable was the fact that they didn't speak to each other.

An implicit agreement that he'd just broken.

She then scowled, no doubt carving an even deeper furrow upon her brow. "Maybe," she replied, her tone clipped. "But, unfortunately, ye are already stuck with *yer* face forever."

Errol inclined his head. "Ye found me handsome once … don't ye remember?"

Inghinn's heart started to punch against her breastbone. *Knave. How dare he allude to the past?* Her lip curled then. "Not in the least … I've seen pigs' *arses* that are comelier than ye." It was a vulgar thing to say—but she couldn't help herself.

Nonetheless, she shocked herself into silence.

What the devil was wrong with her?

A heartbeat followed, and then to her utter shock, Errol threw back his head and laughed.

Dizziness washed over Inghinn. She'd never heard the gruff captain laugh before. The sound was deep and rich, and it echoed over the glen.

Of course, she was lying, for she found him dizzyingly attractive. The bastard *reeked* of masculinity. He was a big, brawny warrior with thick dark hair that fell in soft waves around a strong-featured face, and his expressive walnut-brown eyes had captivated her from the first.

She wouldn't tell him that though—she'd rather have her tongue ripped out.

"Go to Hades, Errol," Inghinn ground out as her cheeks grew hot. How dare he laugh at her?

Errol weathered her fury, his gaze never wavering. "Aye, as long as I meet *ye* there, Inghinn," he growled back.

"I don't know what has set ye two to bickering, yet could ye please cease?" A weary, brittle voice intruded then. Inghinn glanced over her shoulder to find Lady Greer frowning at them. "I have a headache, and ye are making it worse."

"Apologies, Lady Greer … we forgot ourselves." Errol's tone was respectful, apologetic, and when Inghinn glanced his way, she saw that his eyes had shadowed. Like Inghinn, he adored Lady Greer and had no doubt noted that she wasn't herself these days.

Inghinn said nothing. She knew she should also apologize, yet her tongue suddenly felt leaden.

Anger still pulsed through her, as well as a confusing storm of emotions. After years of admirable self-restraint, she felt as if she'd just lost control.

Errol had deliberately baited her, and she'd taken the hook like a hungry trout.

The captain urged his courser on then, moving forward in the line so that he and Inghinn no longer rode side-by-side. His departure was a relief, and Inghinn took slow, deep breaths as her burning cheeks cooled.

Good, she needed to collect herself again, needed to remind herself that they were no more than four days from Druminnor. Once they returned home, things would go back to a safe, settled routine—one where Inghinn and Errol's paths rarely crossed. There were changes afoot though, for soon Lady Greer would wed Malcolm Sutherland and move to Dunrobin Castle in the north. Inghinn wanted to go with her—that way, she'd remain with her mistress and leave Errol Forbes far behind her.

Curse it, why did her chest start to ache at the thought of never seeing him again? Her uncontrollable response to this man vexed her.

Inghinn was still taking deliberate, deep breaths, and wishing her heartbeat would slow, when fat drops of water fell on her face a short while later. Glancing up, she noted that the ominous storm clouds that had hung behind Ben Macdui were now directly above.

A deep rumble followed, and up ahead, Errol's horse gave a frightened squeal and reared up. He kept his seat easily, even as his courser danced on the spot. Meanwhile, Inghinn's usually unflappable mount tossed his head and sidestepped. "Don't fash yerself, Crabapple," Inghinn murmured, leaning forward, and stroking the garron's furry neck. "It's just a bit of thunder."

Another deep boom split the heavens. Lightning forked down between two mountains to the east, and Errol's courser tried to bolt. Only his skill kept it in check.

The rain started to patter down then, just a few drops at first before it increased to a downpour.

Inghinn muttered an oath and yanked up the hood of her cloak. It was a light woolen mantle, made for the summer, and it wouldn't keep her dry for long. Meanwhile, Crabapple gave a nervous buck, nearly unseating her.

"Forbes!" Errol called out to his clan-chief, even as he still fought to keep his horse from taking off. "It's too exposed out here. We should make for the nearest pinewood, make camp, and wait the storm out."

Up ahead, Alexander Forbes twisted in the saddle, his square jaw set, as rain poured down his face. Inghinn knew he'd been hoping to make it out of the Cairngorms today. They'd camped for the past two nights, and the Laird of Druminnor had made it clear to all that he wanted to sleep in a proper bed tonight. However, if they kept riding in this, they'd all catch their death of cold. Aye, it was summer—but up here in the mountains, the weather could turn chilly even during the milder months.

Surely, the Forbes wouldn't risk all their health just to reach the nearest inn?

The clan-chief scowled at his captain, clearly struggling with his advice, before he eventually gave a curt nod. "Very well," he shouted back. "Lead the way, Captain."

Errol eased his dancing courser out of the line and let it leap forward, kicking peaty earth up under its hooves.

In a heartbeat, he was away, taking them north, away from the exposed moorland they currently rode through. Instead, he headed toward a blanket of dark pines that covered the lower slopes of the granite peaks soaring above.

The heady scent of pine enveloped Inghinn as she drew Crabapple up and slid off his back.

Thunder boomed farther down the glen, and the gelding flattened his furry ears back and tossed his head, showing her the whites of his eyes. Inghinn placed a hand on the pony's shoulder, feeling the fear that shivered through him. Many of the other horses here—including Lady Greer's palfrey—appeared unmoved by the storm. However, her pony and Errol's courser weren't among them.

They'd traveled a few furlongs inside the pinewood, making camp in a small clearing that was studded by tree stumps and charred areas where firepits had once burned. Someone else had cleared the trees away here and used this very spot as a camp.

The rain continued to drum down as the Forbes company settled in for the night. Hide tents went up in a tight circle, and the warriors cut down branches from the surrounding trees to create a temporary enclosure for the horses around a large sheltering pine.

"Go inside, and dry off, Lady Greer," Inghinn gestured toward the tent that had just been pitched a few yards away. "The men will bring in our saddle bags."

Greer's pretty features tightened. "Ye should get out of the rain too."

"And I will," Inghinn assured her with a smile. "Just as soon as I see to our mounts."

Blinking water out of her eyes, she took the reins of Samhradh, Greer's palfrey, and led her and Crabapple toward the enclosure.

Inside the rustic wooden perimeter, she started unsaddling both ponies under the protection of the overhanging tree, which kept off the worst of the rain.

Crabapple was still on edge. The poor beast flinched with every peal of thunder that vibrated down the glen.

Inghinn had just yanked the saddle from the garron's back when a gruff male voice, laced with impatience, interrupted her. "What are ye still doing out here, woman?"

Inghinn cast a glance over her shoulder, her gaze meeting Captain Errol's. He was scowling at her, rain running down his face in rivulets.

God's troth, what was this? The captain usually avoided her as if she were a leper—something she was grateful for—yet today, he'd directly spoken to her *twice*.

"What does it look like, dolt?" Inghinn muttered, answering his frown with one of her own. "Seeing to my and Lady Greer's mounts."

"Leave the ponies to one of my men," he ordered, stepping forward and yanking the saddle from her. "Ye are drenched to the skin."

Inghinn snorted, raking her gaze over the captain. She'd been about to tell him that he, too, looked like a drowned rat, yet the words suddenly died in her throat.

The smoke-colored linen lèine Errol wore was soaked through, clinging to his broad shoulders and the sculpted lines of his chest. She could see every bulging muscle.

Heat flushed over Inghinn's chest, and her breathing grew shallow.

She remembered then, a night many years previous, when she'd explored the naked planes of his chest—when she'd tasted the salt of his skin.

Inghinn's legs went weak.

Errol's dark brows drew together then, his patience clearly at an end. "Ye aren't going to argue with me over this, are ye?"

Her chin kicked up, and she resisted the urge to grab the saddle from him. "Enough," she snapped. "Why don't ye let me go about my business, and I shall pay ye the same courtesy."

"Christ's teeth, Inghinn," he muttered, his walnut-colored eyes narrowing. "I swear ye are as stubborn as a mule." He stepped forward, gently shouldering her out of the way as he swung the saddle over the fence. Moving behind her, he then crossed to Samhradh and started unfastening the mare's girth. "I'll see to these two ... now get yer arse inside yer tent before I throw ye over my shoulder and carry ye there."

"Rude, insufferable churl," Inghinn muttered as she pushed her way into the tent she would be sharing with Lady Greer. "I hope a bolt of lightning smites him dead."

"I take it ye are speaking of Captain Errol?"

Inghinn pushed wet hair out of her eyes to find Lady Greer observing her. Her mistress had shed her drenched cloak and was now toweling off her hair with a drying cloth.

"Aye," Inghinn growled. "None other."

Lady Greer arched an eyebrow. "I must admit I was surprised to see ye arguing today ... usually ye just glower at each other."

Inghinn made a choking sound, even as heat rolled over her in a prickling wave. She hadn't realized Greer had noticed the tension between them.

"Aye, well … the man's a boor," she said stiffly, crossing to where a saddle bag had been set down by the side of the tent and helping herself to a drying cloth. "I can't abide him."

"Aye? Why then do I sometimes catch ye watching him?" Inghinn's heart slammed against her ribs at these words. However, Greer hadn't yet finished. "And ye should know that I sometimes spy him observing *ye*."

Dizziness swept over Inghinn, and she clenched the drying cloth tightly. "That's ridiculous," she gasped. "He does not."

"He does … although he's sly about it."

The women's gazes met and held. Greer's expression was open, frank. She wasn't a lass who held onto secrets; she wore her thoughts, her feelings, on her face for all to see.

But Inghinn wasn't like her mistress. Despite that she got on well with Greer, and enjoyed their easy rapport, she was intensely private by nature, a trait that had intensified with the years. She hated others knowing her business and had a proud streak.

Heart hammering, Inghinn looked away first. Lord, she wished they could speak about something, *anything*, else. She'd finished drying herself off the best she could, and now hung her soaking cloak up next to Greer's on the center pole of the tent. "No disrespect, Lady Greer, but ye are talking nonsense now," she muttered. "Errol Forbes is the last man I'd stare at."

Greer huffed a sigh. "Very well, Inghinn … keep yer secrets. I don't have the strength in me this afternoon to get the truth out of ye."

Inghinn glanced in her mistress's direction once more to see that Greer had sunk into the nest of sheepskins the men had readied for her. Her young face was pale and vulnerable, and Inghinn's chest constricted. The lass had been through much in the past days. She didn't want to upset her.

"Sorry," she murmured. "I didn't mean to be rude."

Greer waved her away. "Ye weren't … just exhausting."

Inghinn swallowed hard. Part of her wanted to confide in Greer, to spill the hurt she'd carried around for so long. Yet doing so would get messy indeed. And since her mistress hadn't spoken about the husky blacksmith *she'd* left behind in Dun Ugadale, Inghinn felt embarrassed about being so candid. They were lady and maid, not sisters. It wasn't proper.

After a brief silence, Inghinn took a step toward her mistress. "Are ye feeling unwell?"

Lady Greer shook her head. "No … just cold and damp."

"Well then, what we need now is a little warmed wine to take the chill out of our fingers and toes," Inghinn replied briskly. If they couldn't be honest with each other, she could at least do her job. Despite that the temperature was mild enough, her skin felt clammy and her limbs cold. "Shall I ask for a brazier to be lit so I can prepare us some?"

Greer nodded, favoring Inghinn with a wan smile. "Aye … that's a bonnie idea."

Thunder boomed overhead, followed by a flash of lightning that illuminated the interior of the tent.

Inghinn flinched. A wet, gloomy afternoon had slid into an equally murky dusk, followed by a stormy night. Now she lay on her back, staring up at the ceiling of the tent.

She wished sleep would come, yet despite that her body was weary from another day in the saddle, she was wide awake. Tonight, her mind churned, and her soul was restless. The events of the day had unsettled her deeply.

She didn't feel like herself. Not at all.

Another peal of thunder shook the tent then, and Inghinn murmured a curse and sat up.

Poor Crabapple would be beside himself. She hoped the men had built the enclosure sturdily; the last thing she wanted was her garron, or Captain Errol's flighty courser, to try and break out, injuring themselves in the process.

She'd thought the thunder might cease, yet it rolled on and on.

Jaw clenched, Inghinn pushed her blankets aside. She couldn't lie there while a storm exploded overhead. She had to check on her pony. Pulling on her boots, she rose to her feet and took down her cloak from where it hung drying on the center pole. The wool was still damp, yet warm, from its proximity to the glowing brazier.

Inghinn's attention shifted to Lady Greer's sleeping form.

The poor lass was exhausted. This wouldn't take long; she wouldn't wake her.

Pulling up her hood, Inghinn ducked out of the tent. Around her, the other small pavilions looked ghostly in the pouring rain and the smoking pitch torches that had been erected around the perimeter.

Lightning flashed overhead then, illuminating the pinewood in sharp relief for a heartbeat.

Inghinn shuddered. Fortunately, it looked to be sheet rather than fork lightning—otherwise, she'd be afraid it might hit one of the surrounding trees or a tent. Nonetheless, her garron would be terrified.

Head bowed, she hurried toward the enclosure, her boots squelching on wet ground carpeted with pine needles. The fragrant scent of pine wrapped itself around her as she reached the edge of the trees.

Most of the horses were huddled on the far side of the fenced area, under the overhanging boughs of the large pine. However, Errol's courser was pacing up and down the fence line, eyes wild, nostrils flared, while wee Crabapple, who was smaller than the others, had been pushed out of the group. The garron stood, head up, his stocky body trembling, near the fence. Letting herself in, and carefully closing the gate behind her, lest Errol's horse get loose, Inghinn went to her pony.

Crabapple gave a soft snort at the sight of her, which was reassuring. Yet she could feel his tremors of fear when she stroked his neck.

Taking hold of a handful of spiky mane, she led him out of the rain, shouldering some of the other horses aside so that the garron stood behind them, as far as possible from the storm.

"Ye shall be fine, lad," Inghinn murmured. "Look ... I've found ye the best, driest spot here." Indeed, pine boughs now stretched overhead, shielding them both from the hammering rain. Thunder boomed overhead once more, and Inghinn glanced over at where Errol's bay gelding gave a high-pitched, frightened whinny. Inghinn's brow furrowed; with its long legs, the horse looked capable of jumping out of the enclosure.

Turning her attention back to Crabapple, Inghinn stepped closer to him, pressing herself against his flank. His trembling had subsided just a little. The warmth of the pony's body felt reassuring, and for a short while, she was content to just stand there, stroking his neck and shoulder as the storm continued to roll across the sky above them.

Lord, she'd never witnessed such a violent tempest.

"This will pass soon enough," she murmured to her pony. "And soon ye will be back in yer stable at Druminnor, stuffing yer fat belly with hay. What do ye think about that?"

Crabapple blew hard through his nostrils in response, and Inghinn smiled. "Apologies, lad." She then patted his broad flank. "But ye get fat on just the *smell* of oats."

"God's blood, woman." A male voice shattered her reverie then. "Have ye the wits of a fowl?"

Inghinn jolted in fright, one hand flying to her breastbone.

She twisted then, to find Captain Errol behind her. He'd put a rope around his horse's neck and had brought it under the pine boughs. He now stood next to the gelding, one hand on his shoulder. The gelding's nostrils were still flared, its head held unnaturally high, yet Errol's presence had calmed it.

However, the captain didn't look pleased. A row of flickering and smoking torches surrounded the enclosure, casting a soft glow over him. His dark brows had knitted together, and his strong jaw was bunched.

"No," Inghinn replied tightly once her heart had slid back down from her throat to her ribcage. "My garron is frightened of thunder … I came outdoors to soothe him."

"It's the middle of the night," Errol growled back. "Most folk with good sense are asleep."

"Aye, well … I never had good sense," she shot back, her anger rising. "Or I would never have lain with *ye* all those years ago."

The moment the words left her lips she regretted them. However, it was too late.

A wave of prickling, scalding mortification washed over her. Her tongue had a mind of its own today. Every time this man insulted her, she flung something even worse back in his face. Right now, she wished for nothing more than to dig a great big hole and bury herself in it.

Meanwhile, Errol's handsome face tightened. He then breathed a curse under his breath before shaking his head. "God's blood … since when did ye get such a forked tongue?"

Inghinn's breathing caught, and then something gave way inside her.

Enough. If he was going to insult her, she'd show him an even sharper edge to her tongue. She'd serve him up some cutting honesty.

Leaving her pony's side, she closed the few yards separating them and halted before Errol, raising her chin to hold his eye. She then reached out, poking him hard in the breastbone with the tip of her index finger. "Does yer memory fail ye?" she snarled. "Do ye forget what ye said to me that night … after ye tumbled me in the hayloft?"

Her pulse stuttered as she remembered the storm of passion that had caught them both up. They'd been hungry for each other, after weeks of longing looks and stolen touches. However, the aftermath of their tumble had shattered the rosy picture she'd painted of the young warrior she'd fallen for.

A nerve flickered in Errol's cheek. "I remember all right," he growled back. "I asked ye to be my wife, and ye slapped my face."

A red veil fell across Inghinn's vision, and she stabbed his chest once more, harder this time. "Why would I agree to wed a knave who insults me?"

Confusion clouded his walnut-colored eyes. "I didn't insult ye."

"Aye, ye did," she choked out, outraged that he'd deny it. "We'd barely finished coupling when ye slapped my arse and told me I was a fine field to plow … that ye couldn't believe it was my first time."

Errol's gaze narrowed at this, a flush rising upon his cheekbones. "That was a compliment, lass."

Inghinn growled a curse and balled her hands by her sides. "Truly, ye have nothing but wool between yer ears." She paused then, anger thumping like a battle drum against her ribs. "Ye then followed yer *compliment* by informing me that it was now yer 'duty' to do right by me … and that we'd best see if the laird would handfast us in the morning."

"I was offering ye my protection."

"By treating me like a common slattern? By talking as if wedding me was penance?"

Errol's big body tensed. He stared down at her, swallowing. "That was never my intention," he said roughly. "But ye didn't remain in my presence long enough to hear anything else." His throat bobbed once more. "And when I sought ye out later, ye turned yer back on me … in front of everyone."

Inghinn glared at him, rage still drumming in her breast. Even so, memories dug their sharp claws into her.

Aye, she remembered the incident well. She'd been in Druminnor's great hall, the day after their tumble. Errol had approached her, and indeed she'd turned away, unable to meet his eye—unable to relive the humiliation.

But in doing so, she'd dishonored her lover. As Inghinn had walked away, the jeers of Errol's friends rang in her ears as they mocked him.

He never tried approaching her again after that, and ever since, relations between them had been frosty.

But Inghinn's feelings for the young man-at-arms who'd later be promoted to Captain of the Guard had been anything but cool. Her heart had ached, for she'd been infatuated with Errol for a long while before that fateful night—long before she'd given in to her need for him.

She'd wept into her pillow every night for days afterward.

They stared at each other for a few moments before Errol moved forward so no more than a foot separated them. His face was shadowed this far from the flickering torchlight, yet she could see that his expression was serious. "I've never been good with words." His voice was low, strained. "But back then, I was a callow youth who couldn't believe his good fortune when the prettiest lass in Druminnor Castle looked his way."

Inghinn went still, even as her pulse took off.

Errol sucked in a deep breath before exhaling slowly. "Aye, Inghinn … I was taken with ye … but I messed things up, didn't I?"

Inghinn pursed her lips. She then gave a jerky nod, not trusting herself to speak.

He dragged a hand down his face, murmuring an oath under his breath. "I'm not making excuses for my behavior … but in those days, I had no idea of how to treat lasses." His gaze shadowed then. "I grew up with a father who spoke with his fists. He treated my mother and sister like his possessions. He made all their decisions for his family and lashed out when questioned."

Something deep in Inghinn's chest tightened. "My father was also a bully," she murmured, surprised that she'd admit such a thing to this man. "When I left home, I never looked back. He was demeaning … cruel. Women were only any good for breeding and taking care of their menfolk. Once I was free, I told myself that I'd never let anyone treat me as he had."

Errol nodded, even as emotion rippled across his features.

Inghinn's belly clenched. Lord, this exchange was making her feel as if she were teetering on the edge of a cliff, with jagged rocks waiting to slice her to pieces below. It was beyond awkward, but there was something else she had to admit. "I was soft on ye, Errol … but after that night, I was determined that ye'd never know."

"Inghinn," he murmured, his voice roughening once more. "How I wish I could go back in time and change the things I said."

She sighed, pushing damp hair off her cheeks. "Aye, well, maybe if I'd let ye explain yerself, we could have been friends at least." She was keeping up a brave front when her heart was actually thumping in her ears and her belly was in knots.

Like the coward she was when it came to affairs of the heart, she wanted to run from him and pretend this conversation had never happened.

But to her surprise, he shook his head. "I never wanted to be yer *friend*." His voice lowered, almost to a whisper. "And I still don't."

Inghinn's breath caught. What was he saying?

A beat of silence swelled between them before Errol muttered an oath under his breath. "Curse it," he muttered. "I've always been an oaf when expressing myself … when talking about the things that matter." He broke off then, his gaze imploring. "What I'm trying to say … is that I long for ye … as much now as I did ten years ago."

Dizziness swept over Inghinn. For a moment, she gazed at Errol, not sure she'd understood correctly.

He dragged a hand through his damp hair then, his chest rising and falling sharply. "Why do ye think I've never taken a wife?" he asked. "It was ye I wanted … it's only ever been ye."

Inghinn's lips parted.

Of course, it had only ever been him for her. She'd done her best to deny it and had grown angry at herself whenever her gaze traveled in Errol's direction. Yet her heart knew the truth. The fire that had sparked years earlier had smoldered within her, refusing to go out.

Suddenly, her legs started to tremble and the last of the anger and hurt she'd been clinging to fell away.

Her hand lifted then. Only this time, she didn't jab him in the chest with her finger. Instead, she tentatively traced his strong jaw with her fingertips. "I long for ye too," she admitted, even as fear constricted her chest. She couldn't believe she was admitting this. She was making herself far too vulnerable.

Errol continued to hold her gaze, conflicting emotions playing across his strong face. "Ye do?"

"Aye … some fires can't be put out."

Errol caught her hand with his then and turned it over, placing a gentle kiss upon her palm. "Ye slay me, woman," he murmured. "One look from ye makes me want to kneel at yer feet."

"Don't do that," she replied shakily. "The ground is wet."

A soft, rumbling laugh escaped him, his mouth curving into a tender smile. However, his walnut gaze was limpid, and the way he was looking at her right now made heat pool low in Inghinn's belly.

Lord, how she'd longed for him to gaze at her like that again over the years. She couldn't believe he was doing so now.

But he did more than that, Errol shifted closer to her still, his hands rising to cup her face. The feel of his calloused palms against her cheeks made Inghinn's breathing catch.

An instant later, he lowered his head, his mouth capturing hers in a kiss.

Inghinn gasped again as Errol's tongue swept her lips open. The kiss was passionate, determined, and it made Inghinn's toes curl inside her damp boots. She barely noticed the rain that pattered down around them now. The pair of them were lost in their own world.

Her arms came up, linking around his neck, pulling him closer.

Their embrace quickly went from passionate to wild. Years of longing ignited in an inferno that consumed them both.

Before Inghinn knew what was happening, he'd walked her backward, right against the trunk of the sheltering pine. It was dry under here and private, for the horses that also sheltered beneath the tree provided a barrier between them and the rest of the Forbes camp.

Errol shrugged off his cloak and pushed Inghinn's from her shoulders. Both garments fluttered to the bed of pine needles beneath their feet.

Suddenly, his hot mouth was on her neck, while her hands slid down his chest, exploring. The heat of his body burned through the thin linen lèine he wore, branding her palms.

Errol kissed Inghinn once more, their tongues dueling as he pressed his body the length of hers. She felt the hard rod of his arousal nudging against her belly then, and excitement quickened in the cradle of her hips. Despite the passing of the years, she still remembered just how beautiful he looked naked.

She'd told herself she'd never lie with anyone again, and especially not the man who'd broken her heart. Yet now, all her resolve dissolved like spring snow.

Lord, he felt so strong, so *male*. He brought every sense to life. She longed to join with him again, to make up for all the years they'd lost.

"Ye taste so sweet," Errol breathed as he trailed more kisses down her jaw and throat. "Perfect."

In response, Inghinn gave a soft moan, angling her head back against the rough trunk to give him greater access. Lord, he said he wasn't good with words, yet right now, he was saying all the right things.

Taking her invitation, Errol unlaced the front of her kirtle and pushed both it and the lèine she wore underneath off her shoulders.

Cool, damp air feathered across her exposed breasts. Her gasps echoed through the enclosure when he lowered himself before her and hungrily suckled a taut peak.

Inghinn bit her lower lip as delicious pleasure pulsed through her with each suck. Her breasts, although small, suddenly felt heavy and sensitive. The heat of his mouth and the languid way he pleasured her caused need to coil tight in her loins.

She let her head fall back farther, her eyes closing as she gave herself up to sensation.

A short while later, Errol rose to his feet once more, hiked up Inghinn's skirts, and slid a leg between her thighs, spreading her wide.

Excitement spiked within Inghinn then, a soft cry escaping when his fingers slid between her thighs, gently teasing her. She was wet down there, she could feel it, and so needy too.

Her back arched, her hips tilting forward as she welcomed his questing fingers—and when he slid a finger deep inside her, she started to quiver.

Gasping, Inghinn clutched at Errol's lèine. Mother Mary, she'd forgotten just how good this felt. How had she gone so long without his hands on her?

Errol whispered an endearment and spread her wider still, pinning her up against the trunk. A second finger then joined the first, sliding inside her in deep, sensual strokes, while the pad of his thumb stroked her.

Pleasure twisted hard in her womb, and then she was shuddering, her core convulsing against his fingers.

"Aye, mo chridhe," he crooned as she gasped and writhed. "Let me show ye how lovely ye are."

Groaning his name, Inghinn tugged the lèine from his braies before fumbling with the laces. He'd just worked magic upon her, but it wasn't enough. She had to touch *him*.

A moment later, she freed his shaft, her small hand encircling its girth as she marveled at its strength and beauty. It was burning hot and as hard as granite, yet covered in silky skin—even more magnificent than she recalled.

"Are ye ready for me?" he groaned in her ear as she stroked him.

"Aye," she whispered.

"Good … for if ye continue touching me like that, I shall spend myself."

His hands slid under her backside, lifting her high as he nestled himself between her spread thighs.

Errol worked his way into her slowly, inch by delicious inch, before sliding home with a rough, satisfied groan.

It was almost too much, and Inghinn wrapped her arms around Errol's shoulders, burying her face in the crook of his neck, and breathing in his spicy scent. Moments later, she entwined her legs around his hips, clinging to him as he started to move in slow, possessive thrusts that filled her completely.

Pleasure coiled once more, tightening each time he slid inside. He was touching her in the same place he had years ago, a spot that made her turn inside out. Writhing, Inghinn sought to intensify the sensation. It felt so good, she had to have more of it.

She had to have more of *him*. It had been too long. If only the pair of them hadn't been so crippled by hurt and pride, they could have mended things years earlier. They could have spent night after night in each other's arms.

"Harder," she gasped. "Please!"

Errol grunted before complying. His fingers bit into her hips as he drove into her now, pushing her hard against the tree trunk with each thrust.

Inghinn unraveled. Pleasure pulsed through her, and then a rush of wet heat throbbed through her lower belly. Biting her lip as a sob of pleasure fought its way up her throat, she bucked against him, driving his shaft even deeper still.

She'd been transported that night, nearly a decade earlier, but this was even better. This was beyond delicious—it was everything.

Errol made a choked sound then, as if he was swallowing a cry, and plunged into her once more. His big body stiffened against hers, and he gripped Inghinn tightly to him, his mouth finding hers for a languid, tender kiss.

For the longest time, neither of them spoke.

Inghinn couldn't find the words. The night was still spinning around her. The feel of his strong, warm body against hers made everything right with the world.

Eventually, Errol drew back, his gaze finding hers. It was deeply shadowed against the trunk of the tree as the torchlight stopped short of where they stood, yet Inghinn caught the glint in his eyes.

"Don't ye go telling me I'm a fine field to plow again," she warned, although there was a teasing edge to her voice now. Now that they'd spoken honestly, there was no sting in those words.

His mouth quirked. "I won't," he murmured. "Although … being buried inside ye makes me the happiest man alive." He paused then, his smile broadening. "But I confess, I *am* tempted to slap yer peach of an arse."

Inghinn snorted a laugh. The man was incorrigible. Warmth flowered across her chest and belly, tenderness melting under her breastbone. "We've both grown up, a little, haven't we?" she whispered.

He nodded, and she felt the emotion that rippled off him.

"This is just the beginning, love," he murmured, his hand stroking her cheek. "Will ye object if I propose to ye again? I promise to do so with more grace than last time."

Inghinn gave a soft, shaky laugh, even as her pulse accelerated. "Very well."

She'd answered lightly, as if his question didn't matter at all to her. But of course, it did. It meant the world to her, and her breathing stilled as she waited for him to speak once more. She wanted nothing else in this world but to spend the rest of her days with Errol Forbes.

He released Inghinn then, setting her gently onto the ground then taking a step back. And then, to her surprise, he bent down on one knee on the wet ground, angling his face upward so their gazes met once more.

"My lovely Inghinn," he said huskily. "Will ye do me the honor of becoming my wife? I promise to spend the rest of my days treating ye like the queen ye are."

Gazing down at his shadowed face, she let out the breath she'd been holding, her heartbeat going wild. "I will," she whispered back.

The End

DIVE INTO MY BACKLIST!

Check out my printable reading order list on my website:

https://www.jaynecastel.com/printable-reading-list

ABOUT THE AUTHOR

Multi-award-winning author Jayne Castel writes epic Historical and Fantasy Romance. Her vibrant characters, richly researched historical settings, and action-packed adventure romance transport readers to forgotten times and imaginary worlds.

Jayne is the author of a number of best-selling series. In love with all things Scottish, she writes romances set in both Dark Ages and Medieval Scotland.

When she's not writing, Jayne is reading (and re-reading) her favorite authors, cooking Italian feasts, and going on long walks with her husband. She's from New Zealand and lives in Edinburgh, Scotland.

Connect with Jayne online:
www.jaynecastel.com
www.facebook.com/JayneCastelRomance
https://www.instagram.com/jaynecastelauthor/
Email: **contact@jaynecastel.com**

Printed in Great Britain
by Amazon